ALSO BY A⸻

Nosy Newfie Cozy Mysteries

A Dead Man and Doggie Delights

A Crazy Cat Lady and Canine Crunchies

A Buried Body and Barkery Bites

A Missing Mom and Mutt Munchies

A Sabotaged Celebration and Salmon Snaps

A Poisoned Past and Puppermints

Nosy Newfie Holiday Shorts

Halloween at the Baker Valley Barkery & Cafe

ISBN: 978-1-950902-66-8

A POISONED PAST AND PUPPERMINTS

ALEKSA BAXTER

CHAPTER ONE

As I drove along the narrow two-lane highway towards the only supermarket in the valley, I was not a happy camper. Sure, it was a gorgeous day. Winter, so not exactly warm, but the skies were a bright, clear blue and there wasn't a single cloud in the sky. I was surrounded by the beauty of the Colorado mountains, covered in evergreens and capped in snow. The barbed wire fences that kept the local cows where they belonged off the highway were ruggedly picturesque, as were the farm houses at the end of rutted dirt roads.

A heckuva lot better view than when I'd lived in DC, that's for sure. Then a trip to the grocery store had meant merging onto a four-lane road with only power lines, overpasses, and buildings visible no matter what direction I turned.

Finally, at the age of thirty-six, I, Maggie May Carver, was somewhere I actually wanted to be.

Problem was, it was the day before Valentine's Day.

Honestly, one of the worst holidays on the planet. It's supposed to be about showing your love for someone, but I

1

have to tell you I stopped finding it an enjoyable holiday after about third grade. Prior to that it was all cutesy and fun and I gave ridiculously over-the-top little valentines to my crush—a cute little blonde boy who lived down the street and who I'd declared my boyfriend whether he wanted to be or not.

But after that it started to be about who was popular and who wasn't. And if you gave a *boy* a valentine it was far more than just some cute little card. It was a declaration of war if *that* girl in your class liked him, too. Or it suddenly meant something more than "Hey, you're cute" or "I like you because you're my friend."

And Valentine's Day as an adult? Well, let's just say that for many years I was the woman in black when I bothered to remember the holiday even existed. (Jamie, my best friend, was of course the one in bright pink. Then again, she was also the one receiving more than one bouquet of roses or sweet little notes from her various admirers each holiday.)

But what made it even worse was that now I had an actual boyfriend. Matt was wonderful. Tall, dark, handsome. A good person. (A good kisser.) And somehow bizarrely okay with being with me despite all my flaws.

Which meant I really, truly wanted to erase the holiday from the map. See, Valentine's is easy if you're a guy. You buy a dozen roses or a box of chocolates or a pair of earrings or a bracelet or something sexy and lacy, and you're done. Easy peasy.

Generic as all get out and not showing the slightest bit of thought or personalization, but a woman can't really object if you remember the day and honor it with one of the classic gifts.

Oh, stuffed animals holding hearts work, too, of course.

But for a woman. You don't really buy a guy roses. Or chocolates. Or stuffed animals. Or earrings. Or some little sexy, lacy thing.

I mean, I guess you could.

(I'm now having inappropriate thoughts about Matt and some little sexy, lacy thing that I will stop talking about because he's MINE and you don't need to be going there with me. But he'd look good in it if he'd be willing, which he probably wouldn't.)

So, anyway. It was the day before Valentine's Day. Matt and I were running away to the Creek Inn for a fancy little dinner and a nice night together the next day (which he wasn't going to let me pay for either, taking that option off the table), and I was headed to the grocery store trying to at least find a good card for him.

Which was also not going to be easy. Go with the funny option and he'd start to wonder if I cared enough. Go with the serious, "you're the love of my life" option and maybe he'd run for the door. Or, worse, he'd frickin' propose, which I was not ready for yet either.

Seriously, I think I'd have an easier life if I just never thought about anything at all. But I do.

Which is why I was in a surly mood when I finally made it to the store and located the card aisle with its helium balloons trailing curled string and bright pink and red colors everywhere.

I took my time, reading each and every card, trying to find the one that was lovey-dovey enough to let Matt know I cared, but not too much. (Advice to Hallmark—you need a better selection of cards for the ambivalent among us. And not just for Valentine's.)

I'd just found one that was going to have to be good enough when Mr. Lewis shuffled his way towards me.

He'd been a semi-regular customer at the café when it was still open, although he'd never been much of a talker. He'd come in most days for lunch, sit in the far corner, and eat a bowl of soup by himself. He didn't even bring a book or play on his phone. He just stared out the window as he slowly sipped spoonful after spoonful of soup and then left again, always with a generous tip.

He was a tall man, slender, probably mid-50s, but stooped like a much older man. I'd figured he was sick with cancer or something the way he carried himself, but I'd never asked.

In other words, every time I saw the man I just wanted to give him a hug and tell him it would get better. But instead I always gave him his space and tried to be as quiet and kind as I could. This time, though, I figured it wouldn't hurt to at least say hi.

"Mr. Lewis. I haven't seen you in a while. How are you?"

He turned to me and I could see tears in his eyes.

"Are you okay?"

He shook himself off like a dog shaking off water. "Yeah. I, um." He stared at the floor for a long moment, fists clenched, clearly trying to master his emotions.

I stepped closer. "Is there anything I can do?"

He sniffed and turned back to the display of various stuffed animals piled upon the shelf, their hands clutched around red roses or hearts with silly words on them like "Be Mine". He covered his mouth with his large hand for a moment, pulling himself back together. "Which is your favorite?" he asked.

"My favorite?"

"Of the stuffed animals. I always get her one each year, but I never really know which one she'd want. She's been gone so long."

I desperately wanted to ask who *she* was, but I suspected that if I did he might just break right there and then. And I wasn't sure he'd ever be able to put himself back together again if he did. (I've been there myself a few times.)

I reached for the shelf. "You know, I've always been partial to pandas. And this one here with the big eyes is pretty darned cute." I handed it to him.

"Good choice. Thank you."

He started to turn away.

"Mr. Lewis, can I buy you a coffee or something?"

He shook his head. "No. I'm fine. You have a nice day, Miss Carver."

He shuffled away, shoulders hunched, head down, the panda clutched in his big hand. I wanted to run after him and insist that he let me buy him a bowl of soup or something. But I knew he wouldn't appreciate the interference. And, honestly, I wasn't sure what we'd talk about. We'd never exchanged more than a dozen words at a time in all those days he was coming into the café. That was Jamie's side of things (I was responsible for the barkery), so she'd had far more interaction with him than I had.

Plus, sometimes those pleasant but shallow interactions are the ones you need most in life, you know. Those quick exchanges of a few words here or there with someone who doesn't know what's going on in your life so they can't ask about it and remind you of what's weighing you down. (Or is that just me?)

If I forced him to tell me who he'd lost—because he clearly had lost someone—then I'd become yet another person to look at him with pity. And who needs that?

So instead I grabbed a bag of salted caramel dark chocolate hearts off the shelf for Matt's "gift". I figured even if he didn't want to eat them, I would, and hey, it's the thought that counts. (I'm lucky that Matt likes a woman with a few extra curves here or there. Or that, if he doesn't, he's smart enough not to say anything about it.)

But as I walked towards the checkout, I couldn't stop thinking about poor Mr. Lewis.

CHAPTER TWO

THAT NIGHT IT WAS JUST MY GRANDPA, LESLEY, AND ME AT dinner. They were so cute together, exchanging a quick kiss before they sat down at the table, my grandpa in his usual jeans and flannel shirt and Lesley all polished up and perfect with her snow-white hair pulled back into a classic chignon. Hard to believe that two people in their eighties could be so unabashedly in love, but they were.

I'd been all worried that when they got married they'd move in together and expect me to move out, but the reality was even stranger than that. They'd decided to keep their own houses, since both of them had lived in their homes for forty-plus years and neither one wanted to move.

But during the day my grandpa was frequently over at Lesley's or she was over at our house. They'd have most lunches and dinners together and then after dinner they'd often sit and snuggle on the couch, holding hands and talking softly until about eight o'clock when my grandpa would drive Lesley home.

(Needless to say, I'd taken to spending a lot of time alone

in my room at night. It's awkward to be the third person in the room with an affectionate couple.)

I'd asked my grandpa if they ever thought they'd move in together at some point and he'd shrugged. "Maybe. If we ever get to the point where we can't easily go back and forth."

"I don't understand. Why get married if you're not going to live together? You're basically dating 1940's-style. You could've done that without the whole marriage brouhaha."

(Lesley's family had not reacted well to the news of their marriage.)

He chuckled. "We got married because we wanted to show that we're committed to one another. Also, because Lesley and I both grew up in a generation that believes that if you're going to have sex..."

I held up a hand. "Oh no. Stop the conversation right there, thank you. My grandpa and sex never need to be in the same sentence ever again. Sorry I asked. Carry on. Do your thing. Whatever works for you."

When he started to open his mouth to say something else that I knew I wasn't going to want to hear (or picture) I hurried from the room.

So there we were, almost two months later, with Lesley over for dinner as usual. She'd taken over dinner duties so dinner was fancier than something I'd normally whip up. There were steamed green beans, mashed potatoes with gravy, and a pork loin roast that smelled like heaven. All served in the dining room on my grandma's best china and with the television turned off.

(I have to say I missed the meals my grandpa and I used to eat while tucked up on the old, worn couches watching the Justice Channel, but the food was definitely an improvement.)

When Fancy—my almost four-year-old Newfoundland —laid down at my side and I put her sharing plate on the floor, Lesley glared at us, but I ignored her. That was one fight I was not going to lose in the home where I was living. Fancy got her sharing plate. Period. End of.

She was lady-like about it and it kept her from begging or barking or otherwise disturbing the meal, so too bad that Lesley thought it was barbaric to have a dog eating off of a plate next to the dinner table. She was just going to have to get used to it.

That and a few other things.

Don't get me wrong. Lesley was a wonderful woman. She was great for my grandpa. I personally liked her a lot. But she had some notions about how women should live their lives that didn't always synch with mine, which had caused a little bit of tension. But we had politely agreed to disagree.

Or, more realistically, she would subtly mention her views to me and I would subtly ignore them. Honestly, I figured if I never married Matt a big part of the reason would just be to annoy her.

(I once took this test about how susceptible you are to influence and it turns out I am so unsusceptible to influence that if you actually want to push me to do something you'd be better off pushing me to do the opposite. Turns out I become a brick wall when I realize someone is trying to manipulate me.)

So, anyway. There we were at dinner. They were being all newly in love and gooey while I brooded about the pressure of spending my first Valentine's with Matt and while

Fancy drooled a small puddle onto the floor waiting for me to notice her and give her a bit of food off my plate.

To distract myself from my maudlin thoughts I said, "I ran into Mr. Lewis at the grocery store today. He was buying a stuffed animal for Valentine's for someone, but he looked like he was about to cry."

"Oh. That poor man." Lesley shook her head.

"What happened?" I asked.

She glanced at my grandpa. "How long ago was it? Ten years?"

"Maybe as many as fifteen."

"It could be fifteen by now. You're right."

They both nodded.

"What?" I asked again.

"His daughter was killed. Right after high school graduation. He'd raised that poor girl by himself. She was such a sweetheart, too. So bright and beautiful. And then, just like that, gone." Lesley sighed.

"Never did find out who did it." My grandpa squeezed her hand. "I think that's the hardest part. Not knowing who did it or why. Such a tragedy. She was his only child. He lived and breathed for that girl. He was at every single game when she played baseball for me. When she was in middle school he worked two jobs to save up so she could attend a special summer camp for gifted kids. And when she got into college, I don't think there was a man more proud than he was."

I sat back. "That poor man. I never knew."

My grandpa nodded. "He doesn't talk about it much. He doesn't talk to anyone much since it happened, really. He used to be a tractor salesman. One of the most outgoing and gregarious men you'd ever meet. Always out and about. Always had a firm handshake and a ready smile. But after

Julie died, he couldn't do it anymore. He quit his job. Probably spent the first five years at home, never going anywhere except the grocery store."

"I guess that changed some over time. He used to come into the café for lunch. But he did keep to himself."

"Yeah. After those first few years I saw him around more. He'd nod hello, but it was clear he wanted to be left alone still."

"He was like that at the café, too. He'd order his soup and then just stare out the window, not trying to talk to anyone." I poked at my food, no longer hungry. "That poor man. He seemed so sad today. I wish there was something I could do for him."

My grandpa glared at me. "Don't you even think about it, Maggie May."

"Think about what?"

"Trying to solve that murder. Just because you've lucked into solving a few crimes here or there doesn't make this your business. That man has moved on with his life. Let it go."

But he hadn't moved on with his life. From what I could tell he was stuck in some gray half-life. Ten or fifteen years later and still buying your dead daughter a Valentine's present? It was touching, but it wasn't the action of a man who'd moved on with his life.

Maybe what Mr. Lewis needed was closure.

"Maggie May…"

"What? I didn't say I was going to try to solve the murder. Heck, I hadn't even thought of doing so until you mentioned it."

But now that he had…

Why not see what I could do? Not like I was doing much with my days other than playing too much solitaire and reading too many books. (Not that you can ever actually read too many books in my opinion, but all that sitting on couches or chairs for hours and hours each day does start to affect the body. I had "reader's back" from curling up on the couch for too long too many days in a row.)

"Maggie May, don't go stirring up old hurts. Let this go."

"I heard you the first time, Grandpa." I flashed him my most brilliant smile. "What do you guys say to a game of Scrabble after dinner? You up for it?"

My grandpa narrowed his eyes at me. He knew when I was deliberately changing the subject. But he didn't push me on it. "Sure. Sounds like fun."

"Great."

The whole rest of the dinner I tried to figure out the exact right approach to use on Matt—who in addition to being my wonderful boyfriend was also a cop—to get access to the old case file. That seemed to me to be the best place to start. No use bothering Mr. Lewis about it until I was sure there was something I could do to help.

CHAPTER THREE

THE NEXT NIGHT MATT AND I DROVE THROUGH THE winding canyon between my grandpa's house in Creek and the Creek Inn for our special Valentine's dinner.

Matt had dressed in a pair of nice black slacks and a white collared shirt, the top two buttons undone. He looked stunning with his dark hair and blue eyes and I gave myself a little mental pat on the back for snagging him when all the single girls in the county had wanted him. (Or at least I assumed they had. In small towns your pickings are pretty slim so a guy like Matt goes fast. Not that I'd had any attention whatsoever of falling for him, but when a man that great crosses your path, it's a little hard to ignore.)

I'd made an effort at dressing up, too. I was wearing my one remaining little black dress and had even put on makeup and done my hair, although I'd decided that due to the winter season and my aversion to heels that I could pair it with some cute furry snow boots instead of proper dressy shoes.

Matt, bless him, didn't even mention my unusual choice of footwear. He just told me I looked beautiful, gave me a kiss on the cheek, and handed me a small box of chocolate caramels.

(So many reasons I like that man...)

The Creek Inn not only had a great dive bar (where Matt and I had played pool on what I thought of as our first not-date), but it also had a gorgeous five-star restaurant attached to the hotel portion that was decorated to the hilt for the holiday with red roses and pink hearts and lots and lots of candles.

It was the only place with white linen tablecloths within a twenty-minute drive of Creek. (That's what you get when you live in a town of about a hundred people in the Colorado mountains. Lots of beauty, but not lots of dining choices.)

They had classical music playing in the background to set the mood which was decidedly cozy with about a dozen tables scattered throughout the place. We'd probably been lucky to get a reservation—although we did have an in with the owners, Evan and Abe—but then again, the price point for the dinner was probably out of reach for most of the more established couples in the area.

Abe greeted us as we walked in the door with a kiss on each cheek and led us to a snuggly little table in the back corner. "The best table for my favorite couple."

"Thank you," I told him as he held the chair for me, something I have always found incredibly awkward and honestly makes me want to avoid all fancy restaurants.

(I'm always worried I'm going to sit too soon or not soon enough and make an awkward fool of myself. That and what to do with your napkin and your fork are enough to scare me off of any sort of formal dining, but for the chance at a romantic evening with Matt I was willing to suffer through it.)

They were serving a special menu for the night that included a choice of lobster or steak for the main course (yum) and came with wine pairings, which I love. We each made our selections and then while we waited for the first course I told Matt about running into Mr. Lewis at the grocery store the day before and asked if he knew anything about the death of Julie Lewis.

(I know. You shouldn't discuss death or murder at a Valentine's Day dinner with your sweetheart, but unfortunately for Matt and our romantic evening, that dinner was the first time I'd seen him since running into Mr. Lewis, and I hadn't been able to stop thinking about the poor man since.)

Matt took a long sip of his wine instead of answering, his blue eyes narrowed.

"What?" I asked. "It was a simple question. Do you know anything about the murder of Julie Lewis?"

"Maggie May…"

"Oh, you sound like my grandpa. I'm bored, Matt. There are only so many books I can read and so many games of solitaire I can play. And Fancy's only up for a short walk every day so not like I can take up snowshoeing or something like that. And I refuse to be that person who sits on the couch all day watching TV or lives on Twitter telling everybody how offended they are by some innocuous comment. You have a job. I have…nothing."

"So you're going to dig into some old murder because you don't have any good hobbies? I'm sure Lesley could teach you how to crochet. Or you could volunteer down at the library. Or the YMCA."

"I already know how to crochet."

"You do?"

"Yes. And cross stitch. And tat. And paint ceramics. And

hand-bead things. The only thing I could never get the hang of was knitting. I made the mistake of learning to crochet first and then I always wanted a hook to grab my yarn with."

He grunted. "When did you learn how to do all of that?"

"I must've been bored when I was a kid. But unless you want a cross-stitched fishing scene for your wall for Christmas next year, I'd suggest you don't encourage me to get back into handcrafts."

"So you think we'll still be together next Christmas, huh?" He flashed me a devilish grin.

"Matthew Allen Barnes. I thought we were giving all that relationship talk a little bit of time off."

"It's Valentine's Day. What better day to talk about your relationship than on Valentine's?"

I thought about it for a second. "Pretty much any other day. This day has enough pressure on it as is. No need to go adding a relationship talk on top of it."

He leaned forward. "It's just that there are some decisions I need to make soon and I'd like to know where we stand."

"Together. Isn't that enough?"

"Like the song asks, are we written in the stars or written in the sand?"

I rolled my eyes. "Don't be absurd. If I didn't want to be with you, I wouldn't be. And just because I don't want to talk about it doesn't mean I'm not serious about you. You know I'm not good at all of this relationship stuff. Now can we just talk about murder instead, please?"

"You're going to have to talk about where we're headed at some point, Maggie."

"Yeah, well, not just yet, okay? So, murder. Julie Lewis. What do you know?"

Before Matt could answer, Abe came to our table with a gorgeous shrimp cocktail for Matt and a bowl of French onion soup for me.

"Oh that looks amazing, Abe," I said. "You have outdone yourself. But you and Evan shouldn't be working on Valentine's. You should take the day to celebrate together."

He chuckled. "And miss one of the most profitable restaurant days of the year? Never. February 14th is just a day. Evan and I can celebrate when we go on our Bahamas cruise next week."

"Bahamas? Ooh. Nice."

"It will be. We always try to get away for Evan's birthday. It's the perfect cure for the late-winter blues. You two should try it. Run away for a long weekend together somewhere nice and warm."

I grimaced.

Matt smiled. "Yes, we should. You're right."

I plucked one of the extra-large shrimp off of Matt's plate, dunked it in cocktail sauce, and took a big bite to hide my consternation as Abe left to greet a couple who'd just walked in the door.

(The last guy I'd liked enough to go away with for a weekend, that weekend had ended the relationship, so I wasn't at all interested in trying that again anytime soon. Not even for Matt.)

Next I took a bite of my very gooey delicious soup (which was made perfectly with the cheese all golden brown and melted over the sides of a sturdy brown crock like it should be) before saying, "So? Julie Lewis. What do you know?"

Matt shook his head as he tore a piece of bread off the

loaf in the center of the table. "Not much. I wasn't here when it happened. As far as I know they never had any real suspect. And I don't remember there being any ugly details either, so I assume she wasn't assaulted. Just one of those tragic things that happen."

"A murder. That's never been solved."

"True."

I tilted my head. "I'd figure that must be quite the black mark on your department, not solving that murder…"

"Maggie…"

"What? I'm just saying…Think what a hero you'd be if you could solve it." I took another bite of my soup trying not to make inappropriate noises at how good it tasted.

Matt leaned back in his chair and crossed his arms. "If *I* could solve it. Not you?"

"Well, I could help. But you're the cop after all." I batted my eyes at him.

"And the only one who can get you access to the old case file."

"That, too."

He shook his head and tore off more bread.

"You're going to destroy that thing, you know." I nodded at the doughy clump of bread in his hand.

"Yeah, well. Maybe this isn't my idea of a good romantic dinner conversation."

I winced. "Sorry. Change of subject. Your choice."

"Okay." He leaned closer. "Where do you want to go for a weekend getaway? You want to drive or should we fly?"

Now it was my turn to want something to tear into tiny little pieces. Unfortunately, Matt had already demolished the loaf of bread, so instead of answering I focused on taking a very deliberate bite of my soup.

"Maggie, if you don't even want to spend a couple of days with me how can we plan for a real future together?"

"Hey now. That's...not...fair. I mean, granted, we haven't had much opportunity for quality alone time between Jack living with you and me living with my grandpa, so getting away for a few days makes some sense. But traveling together is tricky. It can ruin relationships."

"So, what? We should never travel together? You know that living together is messy, too, right? Maybe we can have a relationship like your grandpa and Lesley where we never live together even after we're married. Is that what you want? Because it's not what I want."

I huffed a breath and put down my spoon. "No. That's not what I want. I just want a little bit of time to enjoy what we have before we start adding things on top of it that can break it."

He took my hand and held my gaze. "My love for you is not that fragile, Maggie. One bad weekend is not going to break it."

So he thought. But he'd never been alone with me for an entire weekend either.

I bit my lip.

"Nor is one bad Valentine's dinner where you ask me about a murder and tell me you think that going away for a weekend would be too much for us to survive."

"Well, when you put it that way...Fine. What do you think of Guatemala?"

"Guatemala? I think it's a good country for being kidnapped in." He chuckled. "How'd you come up with that one?"

"There's a very beautiful lake there. Lake Atitlan. And last time I was there it had a very beautiful resort right on the lake with a botanic gardens on the grounds. It's one of my favorite places and I've always wanted to go back."

"How long did it take to get to this resort? *After* you flew into the country?"

"Half a day maybe?"

"Not exactly a good weekend choice. Maybe we should start with something a little bit closer for our first trip as a couple. Something that doesn't require shots. Like Arizona. Florida. San Diego."

I grimaced. If I was going to leave Fancy behind for a weekend I wanted it to be worthwhile.

"Okay, so you don't like those ideas. What were you thinking?"

"Iceland? Norway? Quebec? Argentina?"

"For a weekend?"

"A long one. Leave on a Thursday, come back on a Monday."

We stared at each other for a long, long moment.

"See?" I finally said. "Not so easy is it? Maybe we should just sit on it for a while. In the meantime..."

He sighed. "Murder. Fine."

"There are so many reasons I love you." I squeezed his hand and turned my attention back to my soup before it cooled off too much to be enjoyable. Although, with French onion soup I'm not sure that's even possible, to be honest.

CHAPTER FOUR

TWO DAYS LATER MATT CAME OVER FOR DINNER, A SMALL
file folder tucked under his arm.

"What's that?" I asked when I saw it.

"After dinner."

"Is it what I think it is?"

He shook his head and kissed me. "You are a bizarrely
blood-thirsty woman, do you know that?"

I stuck my tongue out at him. "Am not. I'd be perfectly
happy to never see another dead body or photo of a dead
body in my life. What I am is motivated to help those who
can't help themselves. And for some odd reason that seems
to involve dealing with murder a lot of the time."

"So I've noticed. I'll put the folder in your bedroom."

I was tempted to follow after him to take a quick peek at
what he'd brought me, but I knew he wouldn't let me. I'd
always thought I wanted a man who'd stand up to me, but it
was mighty annoying sometimes. Not so annoying I didn't
want it, mind you. Just annoying enough to make me growly
when it actually happened.

I was probably not the most polite and patient

21

throughout dinner. My grandpa and Lesley were focused on the used book sale at the library that weekend, but all I wanted was to be done so I could go see what Matt had brought me. Knowing this, Matt chose to draw the conversation out more than normal until I finally kicked him under the table and he gave me a wink.

"Dessert?" Lesley asked when everyone had finally finished. "I made an apple pie."

"Ooh, that sounds good. But there's something I need to look at first. Matt?"

My grandpa cleared his throat as I held my hand out to Matt.

"What?" I asked.

"This is my house, young lady. I expect a certain level of decorum."

I blinked. "Decorum? Oh. You thought…?" I pointed at Matt and then back at myself. "Oh no. Not with you guys here. No. Matt brought me over the Julie Lewis murder file. I just wanted to look at it. It's in my room."

"Why don't you bring it out here? We can all look through it. Lesley and I might be able to help."

"Okay. Be right back." I ran for my bedroom, hoping that my cheeks were not as bright red as they felt.

I mean, I was almost thirty-seven-years-old. I shouldn't be embarrassed if I was in a long-term exclusive relationship and that meant *relations* with the guy in question. But I have always been one to not want to talk about that. Or acknowledge that it happens.

Not because I don't think it's fine and great and something that people should do when they want and with whomever they want to as long as all parties are legal and consenting. (And out of high school when one of those parties is Lucas Dean.) But it's just not something you discuss.

Ever.

Honestly, the way I blush around those conversations as well as anyone who decides to strip down a little too much, you'd think I was raised a couple hundred years ago. Or Amish.

I mean, my parents were hippies for crying out loud. But I somehow inherited the recessive "let's not discuss that" gene.

Anyway. Let's not discuss that.

I grabbed the murder file and returned to the dining room. "Is this all there was?" It was only about half an inch thick.

"Yep. Well, that and the physical evidence which I obviously was not going to bring here. But there's a list of what's in the box inside the folder."

I opened the file. I'd figured the first thing on the first page would be some big photograph of the body or a smiling high school photo of Julie, but maybe that only happens in TV shows. What was on top was the coroner's report. It was...sparse.

The basic gist was that she'd been struck by some hard object at least three times. The first must have been from the front, because she'd broken her forearm, probably blocking a blow, and then the other two were to the left side of the head making the assailant right-handed.

All clothes were on. No sign of sexual activity, consensual or not. And she was legally drunk, but just barely. She'd died sometime between two and six in the morning.

She'd been found around noon the next day in the woods off of a small pullout from the highway about a mile from her house by a tourist who'd stopped to take a photo of the mountains nearby and decided to let his dog out for a break. The dog had started barking uncontrollably and when the man went to investigate, he found the body.

He wasn't a suspect because he'd spent the night before in Denver at his parents' house for their wedding anniversary where a large number of guests had seen him.

Her dad hadn't yet reported her missing at the time she was found because he'd come home from a night shift at his second job at a gas station and immediately gone to bed at seven that morning. As far as he knew she'd spent the night at her best friend Barb's house. He only found out she wasn't at Barb's when the cops knocked on his door to tell him she was dead.

I shuddered, imagining what that must be like. You go home, fall asleep exhausted assuming your child is safely asleep over at a friend's house, only to be awakened by the cops banging down your door to tell you she's dead.

It reminded me how every single day is the best day in someone's life and the worst in someone else's. Every. Single. Day.

And that poor man...

My grandpa took a sip of his coffee. "He was working that second job so Julie wouldn't have to work when she went to college. Trying to build up enough extra money so she could really make the most of it. She was the first in her family to go."

"And this Barb? What do you know about her?"

My grandpa shook his head. "Never met her. She didn't play on the baseball team with Julie."

"I knew her from the library," Lesley said as she served us each a slice of apple pie and a scoop of vanilla ice cream. "She had a boyfriend she was always with. They were joined at the hip. Tim I think it was? Tall boy. Played football. And baseball. Blonde."

"Oh, Tim Holt. He played for me, too. He and Julie were good friends back then. We called them the Dynamic Duo."

My grandpa coached the co-ed kid's baseball team in town, but it was only for elementary school kids. Once middle school rolled around and the official school sports started up, there was no more need for summer baseball.

"Either one of them still around?" I asked.

Lesley shook her head. "No. Both went away for college. Some small community college. In-state, I believe. Or maybe Kansas. Never came back. I think they got married after college. I can't remember. Tim's mom was a single mom. Always kept to herself. Barb's family only lived here a couple years. They were tied in with the ski resort in Baker-stown somehow, but left after she graduated."

I glanced at the handwritten notes in the file. "Can you read this?" I asked Matt.

He took the file from me and squinted. "Yeah. It says that the night she died Julie was at the lake with Barb, Tim, and a bunch of other kids. There are about ten names here. Julie was supposed to go home with Barb, but started talking to some stranger who crashed the party—seems there were a number of people from out of town who were staying down by the lake where the party was who showed up throughout the night. Barb tried to find her and couldn't. She assumed Julie must have left with the stranger and left without her."

He scanned the rest of the notes in the file. "Cops inter-viewed everyone staying at the lake that they could as well as all of the kids from the party. A few kids did remember Julie talking to some guy, but no one saw them leave together, and the guy's friends all swore he was alone at the cabin when they returned around midnight. He also didn't have access to a vehicle. The friend who'd driven them all up there for the weekend had left earlier that night to return to Denver for some sort of family emergency. And...that's about it."

I grabbed the file back and glanced at the coroner's report again. "And no signs she was moved. She wasn't killed at the party or at the lake. Which is about twenty minutes from her house?"

Matt nodded.

My grandpa took the file from me and thumbed through it. He shook his head. "Not much to go on, is it?"

"Why didn't they do more?" I asked.

Matt gave Fancy a small amount of ice cream on her sharing plate, ignoring Lesley's pointed look before he answered. "How much could you do back then? The internet wasn't what it is now. No social media posts of the party. No cellphone cameras documenting every moment. No text messages. And without sexual contact, you have no DNA. All they could do was talk to people and hope someone saw something, but no one did."

"That's horrible."

"Well, that's sometimes how it works. Even now."

"But they didn't try to figure out who might've wanted her dead."

"According to the notes, no one really had a problem with her."

Fancy smacked her plate with her paw and I gave her a look. She knew better than that.

"Well, someone was obviously lying," I said as I dropped a small bite of crust on her plate.

"Probably. But who? And how much do you push on a grieving teenager when you have no real reason to push?"

I drummed my fingers on the table. "Well, they're not

teenagers anymore are they? And sometimes people realize keeping a secret isn't worth it anymore." I glanced at the file and then back at Matt, biting my lip. "So...About that weekend away you wanted..."

"Let me guess, Kansas? Assuming Barb and Tim Holt live there now?"

"Well, why not? Kill two birds with one stone."

He shook his head. "Maggie May. How about you talk to a few folks around here first and then if we still need to, we'll head over there to see what they have to say?"

"Deal." I squeezed his hand. "You know you're the best, right?"

"I'd feel better about that if I didn't hear you tell Fancy the same thing at least three times a day."

I laughed. "That's different. She's the best dog in the world. You're the best boyfriend. Now, let's put this aside for the night so we can enjoy our pie and ice cream."

As I finished off my slice of pie I was already putting together my game plan. I needed to figure out where each of those kids who'd been at the party lived now and then I needed to re-interview them. *After* I spoke to Mr. Lewis.

That was going to be the hardest part of all.

CHAPTER FIVE

THE ONE DAY EACH WEEK MR. LEWIS HADN'T COME INTO the café was Tuesdays when the Baker Valley Pizza Company had their weekly lunch buffet. (Don't ask me why they only did it once a week or why they thought a Tuesday was the day to do it, but I was glad that's how it worked, because it meant I knew where to find him the next day.)

He was already seated at a table by the window, his plate filled with three small slices of pizza—one pepperoni and two meat lovers. He also had a side salad smothered in ranch dressing at his elbow and was staring out the window as if the rest of the world didn't exist.

"Mr. Lewis." I paused next to his table.

"Miss Carver. How are you?" He smiled at me and I wondered how I'd never noticed that lingering sadness in his eyes before.

"Well, I don't know. Can I join you?"

He looked like he wanted to say no, but he nodded and waved at the lacquered wooden chair across from him. I'd grabbed myself a slice of pizza before I approached so I'd look like I belonged, but I wasn't really feeling hungry and suspected I might not even get a bite in if he was unhappy with what I had to say.

He returned his attention to his meal, like I wasn't even there.

"So, um, Mr. Lewis....I, um, I told my grandpa about running into you at the grocery store the other day and he told me about what happened to your daughter."

He glared at me, clearly wanting me to leave.

"I'm sorry. I know what it's like to have people talking about you after you've lost someone. Like they can't talk to you about it to your face, but they're always right there whispering about it behind you, asking one another what's wrong with you and then salaciously sharing the news back and forth. *Oh, well didn't you know...*"

I shuddered and took a bite of my pizza just for something to do.

We ignored each other for a minute or so, and then I continued. "I, um, I lost my parents in a car accident. And then I lost my boyfriend in a skydiving accident. So I know what it's like. I mean, maybe. I know it's never exactly the same for everyone and none of the people I lost were murdered, but, well. I've been there, you know? With the people, talking."

He nodded. "I'm sorry for your loss."

"Thanks. And I'm sorry for yours."

Such generic words, but how else do you convey sympathy?

We both ate in silence for a few moments and then I finally gathered up the courage to continue. "My grandpa told me they never found who did it. Who killed your daughter."

He nodded.

"And, well, with the barkery being closed...I have some

time available. I thought I'd look into it. If that's okay with you? I don't want to stir up bad memories, but if it was my daughter I'd want to know, you know?"

I scratched at my fingernail as I waited for him to respond. He didn't look at me straight away. Just stared at his plate, shoulders hunched.

"Mr. Lewis? I don't want to do this if it'll hurt you too much."

He fisted his hands on either side of the plate, still not looking at me. "I used to call them. Every month. I'd ask what leads they'd found. I'd ask when they were going to find the man who'd killed my baby girl. And they always told me the same thing. They'd done what they could. Unless someone who'd been there told them what happened, there was nothing more they could do."

He shook his head once, slowly, and his right fist banged softly on the table. "I tried talking to her friends. The ones who'd been there that night. But they had nothing to say. And when I came back again they avoided me. They wouldn't answer the door. They wouldn't answer the phone. They told me they didn't know anything. To leave them alone. To let them live their lives. The sheriff finally came by my house." He choked on a laugh. "Told me I had to stop. That I had to let it go. Move on. Get back to my life."

His hand trembled as he laid it flat on the table. "So I did. I let it all go. Except her birthday. Valentine's Day. Every year I buy her a stuffed animal. She loved stuffed animals, even at the end. Ready to go off to college and she still loved stuffed animals." He smiled softly before burying his face in his hands.

I wanted to reach out to him, but I didn't. I sat there awkwardly and waited, my fist pressed to my mouth.

He met my eyes and I knew that he could see the tears

that matched his. "Do you think you can find him? Whoever did this to my daughter?"

"I don't know. But I'd like to try. Sometimes people remember things later. Or sometimes they don't tell something in the moment because it's a source of embarrassment or they're worried they'll get in trouble, but years later it doesn't seem like such a big deal. And sometimes people cover for one another in the moment and regret it later. There's no harm in trying."

I hoped.

He nodded. "Okay. What do you want to know?"

"Can you tell me about her? What was she like? My grandpa said she was a bright soul. Good at sports, headed to college. That you raised her from a baby?"

He nodded. And then for the next forty-five minutes he told me stories about his daughter. Jules, he'd called her. How it had just been the two of them after her mother passed away. And in every single word I could hear the love and pride he'd felt for his daughter. It made me miss my parents so much, to be reminded of that kind of love and support, but I just smiled and let him talk.

I didn't take notes. I didn't want him to feel like it was an interview. I just let him talk and talk and talk. And I thought about how lucky that girl had been to be so well-loved and to have such a great parent. And how I didn't care what I had to do, I was going to find the sick you-know-what who'd taken that man's daughter from him and broken his life.

Because he did not deserve that. (Not that anyone does.) But it hit me, right there in the chest. I could give this man a measure of peace. I could help him put this in the past and begin to heal.

I could find the answer.

CHAPTER SIX

THAT AFTERNOON I DROVE OVER TO THE LIBRARY IN
Creek to work with Lesley (who was the former librarian
and also knew a lot of people) to track down all of the individuals from the party that were listed in the file.

The library was in a sleek modern brick and glass
building on the outskirts of town and had two conference
rooms and complementary computer stations along one
wall. It was big and airy and modern and I kind of hated it.
I much preferred the old library that had been crammed
into two small rooms at the top of the courthouse and
packed so tight with books it felt like a dangerous adventure
to navigate through the stacks.

Good news was that more than half of the kids on the
list were still in the area more than ten years later. (In the
valley, if you don't go to college, you don't generally leave. If
you do go to college, then you usually never come back
except holidays.)

She helped me put together a list of current employers,
current addresses, and phone numbers and also told me
what she knew about each one.

After that I drove by Mr. Lewis's house. I expected it to be weighed down by grief like he was, but it wasn't. It stood tall and straight, the white fence and the blue siding bright and clean and perfect.

It puzzled me until he let me inside and I realized that all of Julie's spaces—her room and the living room and the outside—were pristine, but that all of his spaces—the kitchen and his bedroom which I glimpsed as he led me to her room—were worn and neglected.

Seeing that made my chest ache, but I hid it from him. He had enough to deal with already. He showed me her room with the trophies and ribbons and class guide to CU still sitting on the desk, the colors bright pink and white and green.

On a shelf by her desk I spied a set of four yearbooks. "Do you mind if I take these with me?"

"What good will those do you?"

"It'll let me see who her friends were. See the kind of things they said when they signed them." Maybe there'd be some mention of a secret a parent wouldn't know.

He shoved his hands into his pockets. "Fine. Go ahead."

We retreated back to the living room where the wall was dominated by framed photos of Julie's smiling face. She was everywhere. If I hadn't known what had happened, I would've looked through that house and expected her to walk through the front door any moment with a bright smile on her face, pale brown hair swinging out behind her.

"Thank you for letting me see her room," I told him. "It helps. The more I know her the more I'll be able to figure out who might have done this to her."

"You think it was someone she knew?"

"I don't know. It could be."

"Everyone loved Julie. No one she knew would hurt

33

her."

I wondered if that was really true. Every person, no matter how good they are, no matter how nice, there's always someone who doesn't like them even if it's only because of how good they are or how nice. And Julie had been a bright star who excelled in sports and academics. She wouldn't be the first to be hated for that.

"I hope you're right, Mr. Lewis. Although that will make it harder to find the killer if it was just someone passing through." I clutched the yearbooks closer. "Well. I better get going so I can get started."

"Wait." He left the room and came back clutching a bright pink journal in his hand. "You should have this."

I held my hand out. "What is it?"

He hesitated before handing it to me. "I had to read it," he murmured. "I had to make sure there wasn't anything in there that the cops would need to see. It was better that I read it instead of them."

He glanced down at the journal, a frown on his face.

"She would've understood," I told him

"Would she?"

I carefully took it from him. "I think so. She'd want you to have done everything you could to find her killer. And she'd understand if that meant you had to read her diary."

He looked at it for another long moment. "Some of the things she said in there...I didn't know...She was so mad at me sometimes..."

I squeezed his arm. "As someone who was once a teenage girl myself, let me assure you, we all say things in our diaries that aren't what they seem. It's a safe place to vent. But from what I've seen here, I expect your daughter loved you very much."

I didn't know if it was true at the time (turns out it was), but I figured she was dead and it was what he needed to hear.

"I better go, Mr. Lewis. Thank you for this."

He nodded, but he was somewhere else, lost in his thoughts, as I let myself out the door and drove home.

I curled up in my bedroom that night as my grandpa and Lesley cuddled on the couch in the living room and read her diary.

As I read the entries, I could understand why Mr. Lewis had hesitated to hand it over. If I were him I wouldn't want to lose that connection to that person I'd known. She was so alive on the page it was hard to realize she wasn't still out there somewhere, dreaming and planning and making her way in the world.

It was page after page of teenage angst and dreams and triumphs. A crush on a boy at summer camp. A fight with her dad. Worries that no one understood her. Worries that everyone saw right to the heart of her. Fear. Excitement.

I knew her dad had probably been hurt by those passages when she was mad at him, but it was right there on every page how close they were. She'd taken him for granted as most teenagers do, but I hoped he'd also seen how much he'd been a valuable part of her life.

I made a few notes. Barb was her best friend, but there was a sort of frenemies thing going on there. Especially when Barb and Tim hooked up, because Julie and Tim had always been so close. She hadn't dwelled on it much, but it was there to see between the lines. A bit of tension between the three of them.

There were other things to note, too. Julie had been

pretty squeaky clean, but she'd talked about how once graduation was over she'd have a summer of freedom, a great time between all the responsibilities and pressures of high school and all she wanted to accomplish in college. The party that night was going to be the beginning. The first time she'd ever tried alcohol.

Put it all together and she'd been a girl looking for a little adventure and taking some risks she'd never taken before with a best friend who probably wasn't going to have her back.

And the worst had happened.

I made a list, too, of all the people who'd signed her yearbook. It was a small class, but it looked like her circle of friends was even smaller than that. About five girls, four boys. Flipping through the pictures I could see that the girls were all friends and three of the boys were, too.

But the fourth boy, Dennis Clay, wasn't in any of the other pictures. No sports. No school activities. His school picture showed a boy with too much acne and ill-fitting glasses whose thin-lipped smile probably hid a pair of braces.

He'd gone to college, but he'd come back. According to Lesley, he'd done it to take care of his mom after a serious fall that she'd never recovered from. She was homebound and he worked remotely as some sort of IT consultant from the home where he'd grown up.

It was only about a mile from the Lewis residence. And in the direction where her body had been found.

He'd signed Julie's yearbook with "love", which made me wonder about his feelings for her. But he hadn't been at the party, so no one had talked to him at the time of the original investigation.

I decided I would. It was as good a place to start as any.

CHAPTER SEVEN

I PULLED UP IN FRONT OF THE SMALL ONE-STORY HOME with green wood siding at the edge of Masonville and took a deep breath. There was no reason for Dennis Clay to talk to me. Who was I really other than some bored busybody digging into events that everyone else had left behind them? But I hoped that maybe that love he'd signed in Julie's yearbook had meant there was some sort of affection for her hidden away that might make him at least moderately friendly towards me.

The place was small but tidy—what I could see of it under the snow that still lingered on the ground. And the station wagon in the driveway was old but also well-tended. So it seemed either Dennis or his mom took pride in their home. That was a good sign, I thought.

I rang the doorbell, but didn't hear anything and no one came to the door, so I opened the metal screen and knocked on the wooden door which still had a wreath up.

About a minute later the door opened to reveal a tall, good-looking man in his early thirties wearing gray sweatpants and a long-sleeved black shirt. I was taken aback for a moment. I knew some men hit their growth spurt after high school and that when the acne and glasses were replaced with clear skin and contacts they were even sometimes downright good-looking, but I wasn't prepared for that to happen right then.

"Dennis Clay?" I asked, trying to hide my stammering surprise.

"That's me." He flashed a grin with perfect white teeth. "And you are?"

"Maggie Carver. I live over in Creek. Lou Carver is my grandpa? I also ran the Baker Valley Barkery and Café until last October."

"Right. The dog bakery. Didn't work out so well?"

"Actually we closed it down because my business partner married Mason Maxwell and they're going to tear all the buildings in the area down and replace it with a fancy schmancy pet resort. So the barkery will be back, but in a bigger and better format."

"Ah. Well. Congratulations. How can I help you? We don't have a dog, I'm afraid." He smiled again. He'd definitely come up in the world since high school.

(Not that I was the least bit tempted. I had Matt. Plus Dennis was a little on the young side for me. But I was making a mental list of all the local ladies I knew who weren't too old or too settled to be interested. I suspected that if he was like other late bloomers I knew he now had all the looks, but none of the moves to put them to good use. Maybe I could introduce him to Elaine…)

"This is a little awkward. But I was hoping to talk to you about Julie Lewis."

He took a half-step back. "Julie? Why do you want to talk to me about her?"

"You signed her yearbook."

He crossed his arms. "She was a popular girl. I'm sure lots of people signed her yearbook."

"Not all that popular, actually. Please? Can I come in and explain why I want to talk to you?"

He glanced over his shoulder. "Fine. But you'll have to keep your voice down. My mother is sleeping."

"Okay. Thank you."

He stepped aside and gestured me towards a nice new leather couch. I sat on the edge of the seat, wishing he'd directed me towards the kitchen table instead—easier to make eye contact that way.

He didn't sit himself. He stood off to the side, arms crossed. "So. Explain what you want. Are you a reporter, too?"

"No." I rubbed the back of my neck. This was going to sound so ridiculous. "Her father was a customer at the bakery. I ran into him buying her a birthday gift at the store."

"Valentine's Day, right?"

I nodded. "He seemed so sad. I mentioned it to my grandpa and my grandpa told me about Julie. And...well...I have some free time and I've solved a couple of murders lately and so I decided to look into what happened to Julie and see if I can't figure out who killed her."

He grunted in surprise and sat down on the other end of the couch, burying his head in his hands. "Why me? Why are you here?"

"Because no one interviewed you back then. At least, it wasn't in the file. You're the only one who signed her yearbook who wasn't at that party that night."

"You think I did it." He leaned back with a soft laugh, laying his arm along the edge of the couch.

"No. Did you?"

"No. But then, why talk to me? I wasn't at the party as

far as you know. You don't think I did it. What can I do for you? Why come here?"

"Well I had to meet you to make that decision. I couldn't decide you weren't a murderer based on one signature in a yearbook. But now I'm pretty comfortable it wasn't you. I figure someone who killed a girl isn't going to sit back so relaxed right after I've told him why I'm here."

He shrugged. "Makes some sense."

"The, um, the other reason I wanted to talk to you was because, well…" I studied the ceiling, trying to find a polite way to phrase it and realized there probably wasn't one and that he was smart enough to know what I was getting at no matter how I sugar-coated it. "You, um, you struck me as the type of guy who was maybe on the outside looking in. And so perhaps saw a lot that others didn't and could give me an insight into Julie and her friends and who might've wanted to hurt her."

He chuckled. "So in other words, I looked like I was a loser who spent all my time pining after Julie and would know everything about her."

"Basically."

He laughed again. "Probably the most accurate description of my high school years I've ever heard. What do you want to know?"

"Who were her enemies? What kind of girl was she? Was she as good as she seemed?"

He laced his hands behind his head and stared at the wall. "She was kind to everyone, including me. I fell in love with her freshman year when some of the bigger football players stuffed me in my locker. She not only made them let me out she got right in their face and told them off until they apologized. And then she went to Tim and made him swear to look after me. Told him it wasn't right for bigger guys to pick on weaker guys. Told him that only losers would do something like that."

"And Tim looked out for you after that?"

"He did. Julie had him wrapped around her finger. Until Barb showed up sophomore year and stole his heart. Or, well, something."

"Something?"

He gave me a knowing smirk. "He was a fifteen-year-old boy. Barb was generously proportioned and generous with her attentions to Tim."

"So you don't think he really loved her? I heard they got married."

"I can't say anything about the marriage. I don't know about that. I think Tim was always in love with Julie but he couldn't say no to what Barb offered. Did lust turn to love at some point? Maybe. Especially after Julie died. I could see it happening. But before that? I think Tim just enjoyed having someone who made him the center of her world."

"And what did Julie think about it? About Tim and Barb?"

He thought for a long moment. "I don't know. I never saw her act jealous. But maybe that's because Tim didn't give her up for Barb. He still hung around Julie just as much as before, he just had Barb attached to his side while he did it. I'm not really sure Julie cared one way or the other."

"And other guys? Did she have anyone she really liked or anyone she dated seriously?"

"No. Not really. Julie was all about sports and school. Her dad sacrificed so much for her, I know she wanted to prove herself to him. She didn't even ditch school on Senior Ditch Day. She and I were the only two seniors in school that day."

"Why?"

"We were taking this elective class on Economics and the teacher told us he was going to give a quiz that day. Said that we could show up and prove how much we valued our education or we could miss class and show that we didn't. You know what the quiz asked?" He shook his head and grinned.

"What?"

"What's more important to you: hanging out with your friends or getting a good education?"

"That was the quiz?"

"Yeah. He was a bit of a, you know."

"Oh yeah. I had one of those in college. Probably one of the reasons I didn't end up a physics major."

He chuckled. "So, anyway. That was Julie. Dedicated. Not all that interested in boys as far as I saw."

"What about girls?"

He jerked in surprise. "Huh. Never thought about it before. But no. I didn't see any of that either. It was just study and sports for Julie."

"Did that shift once she got into college? Or once the end of the year rolled around?"

He drummed his fingers on his knee.

"Dennis?"

"She was a good girl. She didn't deserve what happened to her. That's about all I can tell you."

We heard the sound of rustling from the back of the house and he abruptly stood up. "My mom's awake. I need to go check on her. It was nice to meet you." He walked to the door and held it open for me.

I scrambled to join him. "Okay. Thank you. I appreciate your help."

"Yeah."

I was barely out the door before he closed it firmly behind me.

Interesting.

I suspected there was more that he could tell me, but he obviously wasn't willing to do so and I had no reason to push. Yet.

CHAPTER EIGHT

I DROPPED BY THE AUTO SHOP WHERE ONE OF THE GUYS who'd been at the party, Hank, worked. He was that guy who was probably the lovable joker in high school. A little large, a little doughy around the edges, but always good-humored and there with a laugh.

He shuffled a bit as he joined me in the small office that smelled like motor oil, tucking a dirty red rag into the back of his overalls.

"Boss said you wanted to see me?"

"Yeah, Maggie Carver, Lou Carver's granddaughter." I held out my hand and he shook it. It was just like the rest of him, friendly and a little soft around the edges.

"Nice to meet you. So? What brings you in?"

"Well, I'm looking into the murder of Julie Lewis. You knew her, right?"

"Yeah. Grew up with her. She was good people, you know? Always willing to stand up for the underdog."

"She ever stand up for you?"

He nodded. "A few times. She also stood up to me a few times. I was one of the bigger kids in middle school. I let it

44

get to my head a bit. Until Julie knocked some sense into me."

"That habit of hers ever create any enemies?"

"Nah. Everybody loved Julie."

"Even Tim?"

He grabbed the dirty rag back out of his pocket and started to rub at a spot on his hand.

"Something there you want to tell me?" I asked.

"Look, Tim loved Julie. Forever. More than just friends love, you know what I mean?"

I nodded.

"But Julie didn't see it. Or if she saw it she pretended she didn't. And it worked because there was no one else either. It would've broken Tim's heart if she'd gone off with someone else, but she never did."

"No sweetheart? No crush?"

"Nah. Julie was all about sports and studies. That night by the lake? The night she disappeared? That was the first night she'd ever joined us. Usually it was about a dozen of us down there, hanging out, drinking beers on the weekends. But Julie never came. She'd go to the movies with Tim and Barb or she'd have a game. But when it came time for all the rest she wanted to go home."

"So what changed?"

He shrugged. "She graduated. No more classes to worry about. No more sports to play. She had a free summer ahead of her."

"And she was going to take advantage of it?"

He chuckled. "As much as someone who doesn't know how to take advantage of it can. I swear, she had two beers that night and she was drunk. And then she started flirting with one of those older dudes who'd crashed the party and

Tim lost it. He stepped in and threatened to call the cops on the guy if he didn't take off."

"How'd Julie feel about that?"

"She got angry. Stormed off. Tim went after her."

I tried not to show my excitement at that little tidbit. "You see her again after that?"

He thought about it for a long moment. "No. I saw Tim later. He and Barb were getting into it. I couldn't hear what they were saying, but it was clear she was furious with him. But that wasn't new. She was always on at him about something or other."

"I heard they got married."

He shrugged and put the red rag back in his pocket. "Sure, why not? Julie was gone and Barb was as good as anyone else Tim was going to find. At least he was her whole world."

"Do you think if Julie hadn't died Barb and Tim would have ended up together?"

He shook his head. "No. I'm pretty sure Tim was working up the courage to tell Julie how he felt. You know, one of those 'no chance like the present' situations. They weren't in school together anymore. Worst case scenario, she'd turn him down and he'd spend the summer with Barb and then go away to college. Best case scenario, he'd spend it with Julie and then, who knows?"

Out in the garage someone dropped a wrench and I flinched. "So he wasn't going to break up with Barb first?"

"Why lose the bird in the hand, right?"

"Ouch. So that guy she was talking to that Tim got upset about. What was he like? Could he have come back around later? Or could she have gone to meet up with him?"

Hank glanced towards the garage where another car had just pulled up. "Maybe. I wasn't paying too much attention to him. He was definitely older than us, but not that much older. Younger than I am now. College-age, probably. And good-looking. All the girls at the party noticed him. So he could've arranged to meet up with Julie later. Or could've gone after her wherever she disappeared to. I mean, she had to leave that party somehow. It wasn't walking distance from there to where they found her."

"You're sure of that?"

"Positive."

"Could she have hitchhiked her way home? She didn't live far off the highway."

He glanced towards the garage again, clearly eager to get back to work. "No. Julie wasn't the type to make stupid mistakes like that."

"So you think she might've gone off with a strange guy she met at a party but she wouldn't hitchhike?"

He shrugged. "Well, those are two different things, aren't they? I mean, hitchhiking, while drunk, late at night, along a highway, that's the set-up for a horror film. But meeting some guy at a party and spending time with him? That's life."

(More than one woman had found out that didn't always turn out so well either.)

It sounded like I needed to talk to that guy she'd met at the party.

I wanted to ask more questions, but I saw Hank's boss looking our way. "Okay. Thanks. Anything else you can think of? You ever see Julie and Dennis Clay together?"

"Dennis Clay and Julie? That loser?" He shook his head. "No. Julie was nice to everyone so I'm sure she said hi to him in the hallway or whatever, but I never saw them speak or anything like that. You think he did it?"

"No." Best to shut that one down right away. "He'd

signed her yearbook, so I was just trying to figure out where he fit into things."

"Oh, I could see that. He had a thing for her. Most of us did, though. And she was too kind to shut him down completely." He moved towards the door. "Anything else?"

"Nope. That's it. Thank you for your time."

"My pleasure." He ambled back into the garage, taking the teasing of his fellow workers with good humor.

I watched him go wondering if that lovable teddy bear surface hid anything more sinister underneath, but I really couldn't see it.

So it looked like my choices for the moment were Tim, the potentially jealous childhood friend, and Rick, the older guy who'd dropped in on a high school party and hit on a girl he didn't know. Or, if Hank was wrong, whoever it was who'd given Julie a ride home from the party that night when she tried to hitchhike her way home.

CHAPTER NINE

I MANAGED TO TALK TO THE OTHERS WHO'D BEEN LISTED in the report as being at the party and were still local. None of them had anything exciting to add. Most of them confirmed what Hank had told me. That Julie wasn't the party type. That she'd only had a few beers before she was pretty drunk. That she was flirting with the older guy who'd showed up at the party with a couple friends from a cabin further down the lake. That Tim hadn't taken it well. That they'd stormed off together. That no one had seen her after that, but Tim had come back and gotten into it with Barb, and they'd eventually left together.

So the big question was where Julie had gone after she and Tim fought. Which is why I asked Matt if he'd meet me at the Belgian Cafe for dinner. I would've been happy to fill in my grandpa and Lesley on the case, but wheedling a trip to Kansas out of Matt seemed like something that required one-on-one time. And since neither of us had our own place...

(Something that I had never really had a need for before when I had my own place, oh irony of ironies.)

The cafe was a medium-sized Belgian restaurant outside of Masonville that catered to the tourist crowd and generally employed fresh-faced twenty-somethings from Eastern Europe on temporary work visas, which meant the service was prompt, efficient, and not particularly chatty or interested in our business. Just what we needed.

Matt glanced around as he came to join me at a table tucked into the back corner near a roaring fire. "This was an interesting choice."

"I figured it was the closest to privacy we were likely to get."

He nodded. "Speaking of…"

"Speaking of what?"

"Privacy. You and me. Our living situation."

I'm pretty sure the sounds I made at that point in time weren't exactly coherent. "Why do we need to talk about *that*?"

"Maggie…I told you I needed to make some decisions. And I need to know if you're on board with them or not."

I tensed. "I thought you'd already decided not to re-enlist."

"I have."

"So what other choices are there?"

He laughed. "If you hadn't noticed, I'm living in a two-bedroom trailer with two other adults and a small child. It's not ideal."

"Well you can't move in with me. You saw how my grandpa was the other night when he thought we were going to run away to my room for a few minutes. And he still makes me set the table when you come over for dinner."

"As much as I like and admire your grandpa, I have no interest in living with him."

The waitress came by and I ordered a Coke without

even thinking about it. (I should've probably ordered a shot of whiskey to go with that Coke the direction the conversation was going...)

"So, what then?" I asked.

He leaned forward, trapping me with those intense blue eyes of his. "I thought maybe we could look for a house together."

I'm pretty sure my eyes almost bugged out of my head. "You want to buy a property together?"

"Yes. Since you're not ready to get married..."

I laughed, almost hysterical. "Oh, see, I'd rather get married than buy a property together. A good prenup can take care of most of the issues if a marriage goes south. But *buying* a property together? Oh, no. You have to work together on making the payments and on maintenance and on deciding when and whether to sell or not...No. That's a recipe for disaster."

He sat back and glared at me. "Maggie. I can't do this. You won't marry me. You won't buy a place with me. Has it ever occurred to you that maybe I'd like more than having a few dinners a week together?"

The waitress came by with my Coke and a beer for Matt. I took a deep breath, gathering my thoughts.

Finally, I said, "I'm sorry. That was just a gut reaction. I wasn't thinking about how you'd feel about it when I said it. I told you, I'm not good at this. I'm not good at thinking about someone else's feelings or needs when I make decisions. Or say things."

I put my hands flat on the table and took a deep breath. "So let me step back for a second and think this through."

He took a sip of his beer and stayed silent as I thought about it.

"What's your ideal solution?" I asked him.

"We get married. And buy a place together."

I worked very hard to hide how much that thought scared the living daylights out of me. "Right. Of course. But you'd be okay with us buying a place together in the meantime?"

"Yes."

I drummed my fingers on the table. "What about renting a place together?"

"I'd like to stay in Creek if possible. And there aren't any good rentals available. I checked."

He had, had he?

"Are there any places to buy?"

"A couple." He leaned forward. "But I figured if you were on board with it, that we could approach Roy Jackson's daughter and ask her if she was willing to sell. The place has been empty since her father died and as far as I can tell she's not even trying to rent it out as a holiday rental."

"Not much demand for that in Creek, is there?"

"No."

My fingers drummed faster and faster until I finally forced my hand flat on the table.

It *would* be nice to spend more time with Matt. Especially without chaperones around.

And living next to my grandpa would solve one of my concerns. One of the reasons I had moved to Creek was to take care of him. And just because I'd fallen in love and my grandpa had made it clear he didn't really need my help didn't mean I wanted to be all that far away from him, just in case.

Living next door would be almost perfect.

(Honestly, living about three houses away would be better. Give everyone a little bit of privacy. But next door meant Matt could shovel his driveway for him and he wouldn't have much room to complain since it was right there. And we could drop by to check on him or he could drop by if he wanted without much effort at all.)

I stared into the fire for a long, long moment. "It's a really good idea, Matt."

"But..." He crossed his arms and glared at me.

"What if..."

"No."

"What? I didn't even finish my sentence."

He sighed. "You were about to say something about what if we don't work out. How awkward it would be that I'm living there in a house next to you and your grandpa. And how do we manage the finances if we split. Can I afford a house without you? If I have to sell, who is there that would buy? Am I about right?"

I pressed my lips together. Yes, but now I couldn't say it.

He shook his head. "How is it that you could willingly jump out of planes for fun and quit a lucrative job to move to a small town in Colorado and start a business most people would tell you was going to fail, and yet you can't give us a chance?"

"I am giving us a chance."

He leaned forward and held my gaze with his. "Maggie. Do you really think we're not going to work out? What do you see that I don't?"

"I see myself. I'm not an easy woman to live with. Ask my grandpa. And I'm on my good behavior with him because he's my grandpa. I can be very difficult."

"So can I."

"I can be moody."

"So can I."

"I can be mean sometimes. I don't want to be mean to you."

He squeezed my hand. "Maggie, when you decide to spend your life with someone you can't expect it to always be perfect. We're going to get on each other's nerves. We're going to be mad at each other. Or at something else and take it out on each other anyway. I'll probably leave the bathroom sink full of hair after I shave sometimes. And you'll probably leave too many dishes in the sink. But that's life."

I grimaced. "It sounds very messy and complicated."

He laughed. "Because it is. But if you love someone, you deal with it."

"I do love you, you know."

"But…"

I pursed my lips. "Let's get through a weekend away together before we start putting our credit ratings at risk."

"A weekend away together? Is that why we're here? So you could convince me to take you to Kansas to talk to Tim and Barb Holt?"

I shrugged. "Pretty much. But it will be a good test of our ability to get along for an extended period of time, too. We could drive…"

He pulled out his phone. "Where do they live? Salina?"

"Umhm."

He punched in the location and then showed me the phone. "Eight hours. One way. That's a lot of driving for two interviews."

"Tim is the key to this, Matt, I know it. He can tell us what happened after Julie left that party."

He put his phone back away. "Do you think he killed her?"

"I don't know. If she'd been killed at the lake, I'd definitely suspect him. But everyone said he came back and he and Barb left together. But he will know if she went off somewhere, like with that older guy."

Matt leaned forward. "You sure we can survive sixteen hours in a car together?"

"No. But if we can't do that, we definitely shouldn't be buying a house together. So does that mean you'll go?"

He nodded. "We should make sure they'll be there before we make any big plans, though. I'll call Tim tomorrow from the police station. Make it official."

"You're the best, you know that?"

"I am. And you should snap me up while you have the chance." He winked. "Now. Tell me what you found out so far that makes you think this trip is necessary."

CHAPTER TEN

I TOLD MATT ABOUT ALL OF MY INTERVIEWS, ESPECIALLY the fact that Dennis Clay seemed to be hiding something but I wasn't sure what. He promised to run everyone involved's criminal record the next day. Character usually shows through eventually. How often do they solve some cold case and end up tying it back to someone who went on to kill others before finally ending up in prison, right?

(By my unscientific study of real life cold case TV shows and news coverage I'd say it's about 60% of the time that the killer they finally identify is someone who ended up in prison for other murders or crimes of violence or who was at least suspected in other murders even if they'd never been charged. Then again, I'm pretty sure there are other studies out there that say that people's gut instincts about frequency of events are often highly wrong. But it seemed like a good path to go down either way.)

We did actually manage to spend most of the dinner talking about things other than murder as we split a very yummy serving of steamed mussels in a garlic white wine sauce and pommes frites. (Which for the uninitiated were basically just really tasty skinny French fries.) I loved that I could talk to Matt about pretty much anything for hours on end and never get bored or terribly annoyed.

Don't get me wrong. He's definitely his own person. We sometimes disagree, for sure. I mean, he's ex-military and small town Colorado and my mom was part of the (failed) Great Peace March. But he isn't the type of person who has to win an argument at all costs. Or who looks down on an entire class of people. He judges people by their actions, which is all I think you can really ask for.

So we had a lively discussion, but no active disagreements. And, because life is life, some of our conversation was about TV shows and the locals we knew. (Jamie and Mason were back from their month-long honeymoon in Paris, so we talked about getting together with them at some point. Maybe with Greta and Jean-Philippe—who'd ended up hitting it off a little more than I'd expected at the wedding and were now having a trans-Continental affair.)

Matt and I shared a sweet kiss outside the restaurant and then he followed me home before heading off to his own over-crowded trailer.

My grandpa was just pulling into the driveway when I arrived, so I waited for him.

"You just get back from dropping off Lesley?" I asked.

"Sure did."

We opened the front door to see Fancy curled up on the goldenrod couch. She opened one eye to look at us as we came inside and then went back to sleep. Good guard dog she was. (Although I knew if we'd been strangers walking in the door that she would've jumped off the couch and started barking. She's not an attack dog, but you don't need to be when you're a hundred and forty pounds and have a very loud bark.)

"You and Matt have a good dinner?" he asked.

I took a deep breath. "Sort of. Hey, can I ask you a question?" I'm not usually one for asking anyone else's advice, but I couldn't see my way forward with Matt. I didn't want to lose him, but things were moving so fast.

"Alright. Shoot."

"Over dessert, though." I grabbed us each a serving of carrot cake and we settled in at the kitchen table.

"Lesley is going to lecture me on having two slices of cake in a day," my grandpa said, taking a large bite.

"Just tell her I had a really big one. Or that Matt came over for dessert and had one. But, really, when she makes that good a carrot cake, what does she expect?"

I happen to be a bit of a carrot cake snob. It doesn't keep me from trying a slice every time I run across it, but I have certain standards that must be met to make a good carrot cake. Namely, it has to be moist. None of this dried out brick thing you sometimes get at the store. And not gummy. Don't ask me how to explain that better, but with some places, especially the grocery store, their carrot cakes are just downright gummy. It's like moisture gone wrong.

But the most important, make or break, factor in a good carrot cake is the frosting. It has to be a cream cheese frosting. None of this sugary stuff. It needs to be creamy and tangy and smooth and not leave a lingering sugar film on your tongue.

Weirdly enough, my MBA program served the best carrot cake ever. I would've killed for that recipe. But Lesley's carrot cake was a close second. I could've eaten it for breakfast, lunch, and dinner, it was that good.

The only thing I didn't like about carrot cake was that I

really wasn't supposed to give any to Fancy because of the nutmeg.

I sent her outside with a doggie ice cream instead.

"So?" my grandpa asked, taking a sip of his coffee. "What did you want to know?"

"Well, I guess it's more that I need some advice."

He raised an eyebrow as he took another bite.

"Matt suggested we buy a house together because I won't marry him," I said as fast as I could to get the words out.

He looked at me, puzzled. "Has he asked you to marry him?"

"No. But I've made it abundantly clear that I think it's too soon."

He nodded, thinking. "And what did you tell him about buying a house together then?"

"That I'd rather marry a guy with a good prenup than buy a property with him?" I buried my face in my hands and groaned. "Ah! What am I doing, Grandpa? I love him. But..."

"You're scared."

I nodded and took another bite of cake, savoring the rich taste of the frosting that she'd layered in the middle.

He set down his fork and studied me for a moment. "What would be worse: losing Matt and always wondering what it could've been? Or marrying him and having it not work out?"

I poked at my cake, moving the plump raisins she'd included off to the side and back again. "I know I'm supposed to say that losing him would be worse." I set down my fork.

"But..."

I sighed. "But if I can't make things work with a guy as

great as Matt, then I can't make things work with anyone. So in that sense marrying him and having it not work out would be the absolute worst."

My grandpa took a sip of his coffee and studied me for a long moment before setting the mug down and leaning forward. "It seems to me that if you can't even give a guy as great as Matt a chance, then there's no one you will give a chance."

I looked away. "Good point. Ugh. Why can't life be simple?" I shoved a giant bite of cake into my mouth and gazed longingly at the fridge wishing it wasn't too late to have another Coke.

(It's actually never too late to have another Coke, my real issue was that it wouldn't be a cold one because I don't keep them in the fridge in a failed effort to limit the number I consume per day and I don't like ice getting in the way of my sugar and caffeine fix.)

My grandpa finished off his cake and dropped his fork on the plate. "Life *is* simple, Maggie May. You're the one that's making it hard by digging in your heels every step of the way." He stood up and patted my shoulder. "Maybe you should stop fighting and just let life happen."

I shuddered. "Who would want to do that?"

"Most everyone." He put his plate in the sink and turned to look back at me. "I'm sure you'll make the right decision once you've had some time to think about it."

He left me sitting alone in the kitchen with my half-finished carrot cake and a drooling Fancy who'd finished off her ice cream and come back to see what she could get out of me. I knew what he thought the right decision was. And what Jamie, Greta, and probably the local mailman thought the right decision was, too.

But...Ugh.

Since I didn't want to think about it anymore, I turned my mind to the murder of Julie Lewis instead. I still needed to get ahold of that guy she'd been talking to at the party. His name and former phone number were in the file, but he'd moved on since then.

Fortunately, we live in such a creepy world that one little internet search turns up pretty much anything about anyone these days.

(I occasionally get bored and Google my old friends—or high school classmates who were never friends—to see what they're up to now. I don't find blogs or LinkedIn profiles most of the time, but I do find results that tell me approximately how much they earn per year, what their net worth is, whether they're married or not, what their home address is, and who their closest associates are. It's disturbing, quite frankly, but it is a good way to find out when that girl you really didn't like in high school gets divorced for the third time.)

I pulled out my laptop and looked him up. According to the search results from whatever random sites tell you too much about strangers, he was living in Denver about two miles from where he'd lived all those years ago. It offered to let me pay to unlock his actual phone number, too, but I didn't.

(I had this weird suspicion that the results were real but the service itself was a scam of some sort meant to steal my money. Like those pirated book sites—which I would never use, by the way, because what kind of person steals from a creative like that when there are plenty of free books at the library. I figured half of those sites didn't really have the book but did have a lovely virus on offer that would infect your computer and steal your bank account information when you downloaded from them. If they didn't, they should.)

Luckily, I also found an employer website.

Turns out Rick was an accountant. And reasonably good-looking as the witnesses had mentioned. But he also looked a bit like a jerk. You know that spoiled kind of guy who has always had someone there to bail him out of trouble? They always seem to have this "I'm the man" vibe to them? Well, he definitely had it. I can't describe it, it's something in the tilt of the chin or the quirk of the lip.

Whatever it was, I really didn't like him as soon as I saw his photo.

I was willing to bet he'd have some postcard-perfect picture somewhere on his desk with his attractive blonde wife and two adorable children, all of them in matching clothes that involved khaki and bright pastels, seated on a perfectly green lawn.

And he'd be a golfer, too.

Only question was, was he the type to kill some teenage girl he chatted up at a party? Could be. I could see a scenario where she started something she didn't want to finish, he forced the point, and then got scared she'd tell someone about it and killed her to keep her quiet. But there hadn't been signs of that on the body.

So what would it be? He drove her home and on the way home tried something and she ran and he went after her?

No. That kind of guy was a coward at heart. If she'd run he'd've just left her and gone back to his cabin. Plus he supposedly didn't have access to a car that night.

Which meant as much as I didn't like his appearance, he probably wasn't my killer. But he still might know something useful. Matt and I could drop in on him on the way to

Kansas or the way back. I wanted to see his face when I talked to him. So much of communication is about body language and not the words someone actually says.

With that cheery plan in place, I went to bed. But I didn't sleep well. Stupid love and all its stupid complications.

CHAPTER ELEVEN

THE NEXT DAY I DROPPED BY THE POLICE STATION TO SEE Matt and the results of the reports he'd pulled on everyone. It was just down the street from my grandpa's house and the weather was decent enough that I chose to walk.

I tried to take a moment and breathe in the clear, crisp air and appreciate the beauty that comes with living in a small town in the Colorado mountains. Creek wasn't big—about forty homes total, half of those converted mobile homes—which meant it was nice and quiet, no ambulances or fire trucks speeding by to disturb the peace.

Some would probably find it boring, but I found it refreshingly peaceful.

The police station was a single-story brick building with just a handful of jail cells. Most people who had to be in jail there didn't stay long before they were transferred out or released. Marlene, who manned the front desk gave me a quick smile and wave as I stepped inside.

Matt was tucked away at his desk, no sign of Officer Clark who shared the desk facing his nor of the cops who used the other two desks on the opposite side of the room. I could see someone in one of the glassed-in offices behind that, but otherwise the place was quiet as a tomb.

I shuddered at the memory of the interrogation room that was down the hall past that as well as the holding cells. One night there had been enough for me for a lifetime.

Matt waved me over with a big smile. "Ben's off today, so you can use his seat."

"Are you sure he won't psychically sense that I was here and arrest me for it later?" I asked, not entirely joking. (He had it in for my family.)

Matt shook his head and held out a small stack of paper. "Here you go. Three hits. You want me to grab you a Coke?"

"Yes, please," I beamed at him as I thought once more about how he was the best boyfriend in the world.

(What? Other women like diamonds and furs, I like Coca-Cola and a man who doesn't judge my choice of footwear.)

I thumbed through the pages and frowned.

You know what they say about assuming you can judge people by appearances? Well, seems I was bad at it. Because when Matt finally pulled the criminal records for all of the individuals tied to Julie Lewis, two of the three with any sort of record were Dennis Clay and Hank.

Hank it seemed had a history of getting drunk and punching things. And people. No lovable teddy bear after all, but a belligerent angry drunk who'd been arrested on more than one occasion and had even thrown a couch off a ten-story balcony when he was in college. (Which happened to end his college football career.)

And Dennis Clay had a restraining order filed against him by a girl in his dorm freshman year of college who said he'd followed her around everywhere and made her feel uncomfortable. A girl he'd never dated, just had an infatuation with.

I figured it had to be pretty bad if she'd felt the need to file an actual restraining order with the cops for it rather than just deal with it through campus housing or by peer pressure on him to knock it off.

(Not that I think that's the ideal way to handle things. It's more that most women hesitate quite a bit to make something like that "official" so I'd expect a woman who wasn't in fear for her life would've exhausted all other options first.)

"What's wrong?" Matt asked as I stared at the reports.

"Dennis just seemed like such a nice guy when I met him. I mean, sure, I saw that socially awkward thing in his yearbook photo, but he seemed decent when I met him. I was going to try to fix him up with Elaine. And now to find out he's a creepy stalker..."

"Maybe he's learned his lesson since then. There was no allegation of physical violence, just not knowing how to walk away when someone wasn't interested."

I rolled my eyes. Leave it to a man to say that. "They granted a restraining order against him, Matt."

"Let me check something." He turned to his computer and typed away for a bit, humming to himself as he looked at this or that, moving things around with his mouse, his eyes lighting up as he hit print a few more times.

"Well? What are you finding?" I finally asked.

He handed me the printouts with a triumphant smile. "Mitigation."

"Care to explain?"

"There was a dropped assault charge filed by the woman when she was in high school. I followed that trail and found that the man who'd been charged—who was her boyfriend at the time—was later sent away for five years for beating a different girlfriend into a coma. And some other things around her family indicate that maybe she came from a pretty rough background."

"So?"

"So…maybe—don't yell at me for it—this was a woman who expected men to be dangerous. So when Dennis followed her around she didn't see it as a harmless infatuation, even though that's what it was."

I threw the pages on the table and crossed my arms. "It's still creepy to have some guy follow you around. I had some guy do that to me at a job I had in college and it made me physically ill to go into work with him."

"But did you think he was going to harm you?"

I sighed. "No. Being socially awkward and creepy is not the same as being dangerous. Although I just feel so disappointed with Dennis now to find that out about him. And I really don't like to excuse that kind of behavior even when it's not dangerous. People should know better."

"You're investigating a murder, Maggie. You have to be able to separate out awkwardly unlikeable people from dangerous people."

Rather than go on a feminist rant about how men rarely have to deal with this kind of crud (that was not the word I used in my mind), I just glared at the desk for a long moment before I spoke again. "Fine. So Hank and Dennis stay on the list as suspects because of their records. But really, we're no closer to finding our killer than when we started. Which means Denver and Salina this weekend."

Matt nodded as I read through the last record he'd found. It was for Amy Haverson, a friend of Barb and Julie's who'd been at the party. Unfortunately, there was going to be no interviewing her. She'd taken a quick and ugly turn towards hard core drugs after high school that had led to homelessness and ultimately killed her five years later.

But I did wonder why she'd taken such a downward turn. Maybe she'd witnessed the murder. Or committed it.

But how was I going to prove it?

Honestly. Coming up with new dog treats was so much easier than investigating murder. Too bad there were only so many I could come up with. Although I was almost done perfecting the recipe for my latest treat: Puppermints. Very witty, don't you think? And very minty, too.

CHAPTER TWELVE

MATT CAME TO MY HOUSE AT NINE IN THE MORNING ON Saturday for our drive to Kansas. We'd decided we'd drive to Salina that day, interview Tim and Barb on Sunday, drive back to Denver that night, and then interview Rick on Monday before heading home.

Three whole days together.

Lots of it in a closed, cramped space. I mean, not really that closed and cramped. It's not like we were driving a two-seater convertible or something. We were actually taking my van which was reasonably roomy.

It just *felt* like it was going to be an incredibly small space since all the expectations for our future were coming along for the ride.

(I know. I was pathetic. One of the many, many reasons I'd stayed single for as long as I had. Most men weren't worth the mental gymnastics I went through to date them.)

Fancy ran to the door when I grabbed my rolling suitcase and looked at me with her big amber eyes.

"You have to stay here, kiddo."

She stared at me like I was breaking her heart.

"It's just a few days."

She ran to where her leash was hanging and back over to me. For someone who couldn't talk she certainly knew how to communicate.

"I took you for a walk this morning. Specifically because I knew I was going to have to leave you behind. You'll be fine. Grandpa will give you lots of treats."

She continued to stare at me, all eager anticipation.

"Come here." I led the way into the kitchen and gave her a doggie ice cream. She ran outside to lay in a snowbank and eat it as I hurried back to the front door where Matt was waiting.

"Let's get out of here before I start trying to figure out how to bring her along. I've got the suitcase, you grab the two cases of Coke and the cooler."

"Two cases of Coke? For three days?"

"I drink more Coke when I'm stressed." I led the way to the van and threw my suitcase in the back. "I'll probably only need four a day, but why risk running out? Plus, you might actually want one for yourself."

Matt looked like he wanted to say more about my addiction, but he just set the cooler and two cases of Coke in the back next to my suitcase before grabbing his bag from his vehicle. "Okay, then. Let's get this party started. Who's driving?"

I blinked. "Well, it is my van…"

"True."

"But you want to drive don't you?"

He shrugged. "Whatever you want."

"Oh no. That's not going to last the whole trip. You better have some opinions, buddy, or you're not going to survive the next three days."

He raised an eyebrow at me. "Is that so?"

"It is. I'd rather you legitimately disagree with me than have no wants or needs of your own. But I'm going to drive."

He laughed. "You are, are you? I thought you wanted me to have opinions."

"I do. But I can't drive in Kansas. So I'll drive to the border and then you can take over."

As we got into the van he asked, "Why can't you drive in Kansas?"

I grimaced, remembering the last time I'd passed through and been pulled over within ten minutes of crossing the border. "They're on top of speeders like nobody's business and I don't want a ticket." (Another one.) "So since you drive slower than my grandma, you can drive in Kansas, I'll drive in Colorado."

"A strange solution, but I think it works."

Relationship test one, passed.

Before we pulled out of the driveway I hooked up my ancient iPod through the cigarette lighter. (I had an old van.) "What music do you want to listen to?"

"No talk radio?"

"No. I want to enjoy this drive not imagine creative ways to kill myself or the rest of the world." I handed him the iPod and started the van. "Figure it out. Pretty much anything on there I'm willing to listen to."

He scrolled through. "Greek music?"

"Okay, almost anything on there."

"Thai language lessons?"

"Matt…"

"You did say pretty much anything on here. And I've always wanted to learn Thai." He flashed me a wicked grin.

"Very funny. And before you go there, let's skip the French language lessons, classical music, and opera, too.

They were phases I was going through, but none of them really stuck."

"Yes, ma'am. I think this playlist will work."

As the sounds of a Blood, Sweat, & Tears song started, I nodded my head. "That will definitely work. Congratulations, Matthew Allen Barnes, you have passed couple-road-tripping-together tests numbers one and two."

"And we're not even out of the driveway yet." He leaned back. "How many tests are there?"

"I don't know, but it's a lot. Hand me a Coke, please?"

Matt raised an eyebrow, but he grabbed me a Coke from the cooler and even opened it for me. "Test number three? Will you give your girlfriend a Coke without making a comment when she asks for it way too early in the morning?"

"Sure, why not, since you passed that one, too. Although barely." I took a sip of the Coke and placed it in the cup holder before backing out of the driveway.

As I turned onto the highway I silently prayed to whoever might be listening that we'd be as comfortable together when we returned as we were right then.

CHAPTER THIRTEEN

We stopped for an early lunch in Arvada. There was this incredibly good little family-owned Italian place I knew right off the highway. It only had six tables in the whole place and was hidden away in a little strip mall, but they made the best calzone in the world and I wasn't about to miss the chance to have lunch there if it presented itself.

"I have to agree that was a delicious calzone," Matt said, polishing off his half of the meatball calzone we'd ordered. (The things were so big there was no point in ordering one for each of us.)

I grinned. "I think that's road tripping test number ten passed, then."

Seeing the slight tightening around his eyes, I reached across the table and squeezed his hand. "And now I stop mentioning that from here on out because it's no longer funny, is it?"

"Not particularly."

I took a sip of my soda and tried to think of a way to ease the tension. "What was your impression of Tim Holt when you talked to him?"

"Nice guy. Happy to help with anything we needed. He's a school teacher, you know."

"Really? I didn't see that coming."

"Middle school science."

"Not exactly the type of guy you'd think could be a killer." I glanced at the menu, tempted to order dessert but then decided against it and instead waved for the check.

"Nope. Not at all."

"And Barb? They're still together?"

He nodded. "I don't know what she does. Maybe stays home with the kids. There was some tension there when he mentioned Barb. Not sure what caused it. He said he'd make sure she was there when we came by, but I had the distinct impression it would mean a fight to make it happen."

The waiter brought over the check and Matt handed over a credit card before I could even reach for my purse. He gave me a look that made it clear I wasn't going to be paying for a single meal the whole weekend.

I pursed my lips and sat back, choosing to just accept it since I secretly liked it anyway. "Interesting. Could be that Julie's death has always put strain on their relationship, so he's not looking forward to telling Barb the cops are investigating it again."

"Could be." The waiter brought back the slip and Matt signed it. He glanced at the last couple of bites left on my plate. "You ready to get back on the road?"

"I am." I regretted not finishing every single bite, but I was stuffed to the gills. That's okay, I'd forgotten that I now had a boyfriend. Matt quickly finished off the little bit I'd left and held the door for me as we made our way back out to the van.

As I settled into the driver's seat, I thought about how I

actually liked road trips. I liked driving down a nice flat highway with my music playing, letting my thoughts wander where they may. But it was an adjustment to have someone in the car with me. Not a bad one per se, just an adjustment.

Fortunately, like I said before, Matt and I can talk for hours and get along just fine.

"So," I said, as we pulled back onto I-70. "Tell me what foreign country you'd most like to visit and why..."

And so it went for the next six hours of driving across the very, very flat and boring plains of Colorado and Kansas.

(If you've never been there picture flat plains that stretch in all directions, cover them with snow, and have the only mountains anywhere nearby in your rearview mirror and you'll have an idea of what most of that drive was like. It was just Matt, me, and the semis all driving a little faster than we should.)

(Until we hit Kansas and Matt took over and drove at exactly one below the speed limit the rest of the way. I guess every guy has to have a flaw. Or in this case, an advantage, since we passed three cops along the way.)

I was glad the weather was good, because when the winter storms really get going they close the gates across the highway and you aren't going to get anywhere until that particular storm is past. And as much as I liked Limon, I didn't really want to get stuck there.

It was almost dark by the time we pulled into the parking lot of the La Quinta. I knew it well. I'd stayed there with Fancy on the way to Colorado. It was dog-friendly, which is always my biggest criteria when traveling with her. We'd passed through in the summer so the place had been full of travelers and their dogs and their RVs. This time around I wondered if Matt and I were the only guests in the place.

It didn't matter, though. We just needed somewhere serviceable to lay our heads for the night, which it definitely was. Although it did make me miss my girl. But one quick call to my grandpa who assured me she was fine and all was good.

CHAPTER FOURTEEN

THE NEXT DAY WE MET TIM AND BARB HOLT AT THEIR house. There were half a dozen different kids' bicycles scattered across the lawn even though it was winter and you'd think there wouldn't be any need for bikes. But from the look of the place they could've been left there in the summer.

It was nice enough. Two stories with a combination of brick and wood paneling, painted an odd shade of yellow that was almost mustard yellow but not quite. It showed its age in the cracked driveway and faded wood around the windows, but overall it was a home I could see myself being fine with. (Except for the color.)

Tim answered the door with a toddler on his hip of indeterminate gender. The kid was cute. Lots of curly blonde hair flopping into his or her eyes and wearing a white t-shirt with a koala and red stains on it. Tim looked much like he had in high school with blonde hair and an athlete's build.

"Hey there. Sorry for the chaos. Babysitter will be here in a few." He held out a hand to shake. "Tim Holt."

"Matt Barnes."

"Maggie Carver."

We each shook his hand.

"Any relation to Lou Carver?" Tim asked as he shook my hand.

"My grandpa."

"Great man. Best times of my life were playing baseball for him. He's the reason I ultimately got a scholarship to play in college. Come in." He turned back towards the living room. "Barb's in the kitchen, feeding the rest of the kids a snack. I swear, they're like locusts. They'll eat anything and everything if given the chance."

The living room was much like the front lawn. There were plastic toys everywhere and I wondered how Tim could brave walking barefoot through that mess. Me I'd be wincing in anticipation of a Lego brick in the bottom of the foot with each step. But not only did he do it with ease, he somehow managed to do so without stepping on a single toy along the way.

(I wasn't quite so lucky. Fortunately, the hard piece of plastic I stepped on didn't break, just turned my ankle a bit.)

I glanced around. School pictures covered the walls along with one wedding photo of Tim and Barb where they looked like kids themselves.

"How many kids do you have?" I asked.

"Five. Numbers three and four were unexpected twins. And number five was simply unexpected. But we get by. And it's great to have all these little guys running around. Can't wait until they're a little older and I can teach them all how to build a model volcano."

"Tim. Get in here. I need your help," a woman's voice snapped from the other room.

Tim grimaced and moved towards the kitchen, the kid still balanced on his hip.

After he'd disappeared around the corner I glanced at Matt. "You don't want five kids do you? Or even three?"

"I don't know. It's kind of a fun idea to have your own basketball team."

"Matt…"

He tugged my ponytail. "Five? No. But at least one or two."

"You know I'm old. That might not happen."

"You're not that old. You're not even forty."

I shook my head. "Hey, just because celebrities make it happen when they're like fifty does not mean that most of us mere mortals can. I'm already in the geriatric pregnancy stage."

"Geriatric?" He laughed, but I nodded.

He looked a little more somber as he said, "All I ask is that you're willing to try. Are you willing to try?"

My gut clenched. Marriage was one thing. Kids? That was taking responsibility for the molding of another human being. For eighteen years. And then being there forever for them. I liked the idea of being really old and having a bunch of grandkids running around for the holidays. It was the in between step I wasn't particularly interested in.

(Don't get me wrong. I think kids are great. They're fascinating little bundles of contradiction and strange questions. And just adorable in general up to a certain age. But it's like puppies. They're cute to look at, but hell to raise.)

"Maggie? Are you willing to have kids?" The look he gave me was so intent I wouldn't have been surprised if he was reading my soul.

I inhaled deeply. "In for a penny, in for a pound, right? Which means that if I agree to marry you, I'll agree to have kids. We'll need something to bind us together for all those years after all."

"Our love won't be enough?"

I shrugged. "It better be if we can't have kids."

I wasn't going to explain to him how impossibly crazy I think it is to expect two people to live parallel lives for that long if they don't have kids or a business or a common purpose that keeps them somewhat on the same path. No need to put even more pressure from my craziness on what was already a fragile situation.

The doorbell rang. I'd never been more glad for an interruption in my life.

Tim came back, a different child balanced on his hip, this one in a panda t-shirt but otherwise much like the first one. "That'll be the babysitter. Hopefully. Either that or a Jehovah's Witness. And if it is a Jehovah's Witness, man are they going to be surprised when I thrust Pam into their arms."

Fortunately for the imaginary Jehovah's Witnesses—because they always seem to come in pairs, don't they?—it was the babysitter. A teenager with braces and freckles who quickly managed to lead the little troupe of kids up the stairs with promises to play at least three different games, none of which I recognized. She had Pam tucked onto her hip, the other matching toddler gripped by the hand, and a girl of about eight trailing along behind with a baby in her arms as she herded a boy of about five ahead of her.

"Wow." That's really all I had to say about that.

Matt caught my eye and grinned. "Like I said, a basketball team…Could be fun…"

CHAPTER FIFTEEN

WE SETTLED DOWN IN THE KITCHEN. BARB OFFERED US both a beer even though it was only eleven in the morning. She'd clearly already had at least one herself. It was hard to tell whether it was the booze or the babies that had aged her so fast, but where Tim looked much like the kid he'd been in high school she looked like a worn-out version of someone my mother's age.

She plopped down in a chair across from us. "Tim said you're looking into Julie's murder."

"We are," I answered.

"Well, don't know what we can tell you." She took another sip of beer. "She went to that party and then disappeared and then they found her body. That's all we know."

"You were supposed to be her ride home that night, weren't you?" I asked.

"Yeah. Wasn't our fault she wasn't around when it was time to go. Probably off with that older dude she'd been flirting with." Barb slanted a glance towards Tim who'd hunched his shoulders at her bitter tone.

"I wanted to wait for her," he mumbled.

"No point when she wasn't going to have any interest in leaving. And I wasn't going to stick around while she got it on with that dude."

"Is that where she went? Are you guys sure?" I asked.

Tim nodded.

"That wasn't clear in the police report."

He stood up and grabbed himself a beer from the fridge. "We told them about the guy. They talked to him, didn't they?"

"They did. But you didn't tell them you were sure that's where she'd gone. You just said they'd talked at the party."

He took a long swig of beer.

Matt leaned forward. "Can you tell us what happened that night?"

Tim stayed standing by the fridge. "Not much to tell. Julie came to the party with us. Some guys we didn't know showed up. She started talking to one of them. They left together."

"That's not what we heard. We heard *you* got in a fight with her." Matt focused on Tim with a laser-like intensity that made even me squirm.

Tim took another long swig of his beer. "So I said some things to her before she left. I didn't like the look of the guy."

"You didn't like the look of him, but you let her leave with him?" I could almost feel the intense spotlight of Matt's gaze as he focused on Tim.

"It wasn't like that. It was…" Tim sat down at the table and ran his hand through his hair.

Barb sat back, arms crossed, a sneer on her face. "Go ahead. I know how you felt about her, don't I?"

He stared at a spot in the center of the table. "Julie came to the party with us. It was the first time she'd been to a party like that. First time she'd had anything to drink. And then she's all tipsy and this guy shows up and he's all into her and she's giggling and flirting back. I told him to leave. I told him I'd call the cops because he wasn't invited and it wasn't his property. And he left."

"Alone?" Matt asked.

"Alone. And then Julie turns on me and starts screaming at me that I had no right to do that. That she could make her own decisions." He shook his head, clearly disagreeing even all those years later.

"What happened next?"

"She stormed off." He crossed his arms.

"And?"

We waited as Tim worked the metal tab loose from his beer can. "And I went after her. We...said some things."

"Oh just tell them, would you?" Barb finished her beer and crumpled it up before throwing it towards the trash can. (She missed.) "You went after her and confessed your love for her. Told her you were looking out for her because you didn't want her to get hurt. Because you loved her and always had. Because she was the only one for you."

I glanced back and forth between the two of them. Tim wasn't surprised by what she said. "Were you there, Barb? Or did he tell you about it later?" I asked.

"I was there. I followed after them. Got close enough I could hear the whole sorry mess. But here's what matters." She rested her forearms on the table and it shifted under her weight. "When Tim was done, Julie left to go after that guy. Tim and I left the party together. She was fine when we left. And we never saw her again."

"That true?" Matt asked.

Tim rubbed at the back of his neck. "Yeah. Julie left, headed in the direction of that guy's cabin, and we went home without her." He downed the last of his beer and stood to throw it and Barb's in the trash can.

"Where'd you go?" I asked.

"My house," Tim said.

"Yeah, we had to kiss and make up," Barb sneered.

I glanced at Matt, but he shrugged. "Okay then. Thank you. We appreciate the time."

We made our awkward goodbyes and got out of there as fast as we could. Nothing more we were going to get out of them and I desperately wanted to get away from that lovely example of marital bliss.

As he merged his way onto I-70, Matt finally spoke, "I don't think we'd ever be like that, Maggie, no matter how bad things got."

"No? Do you think they were like that when they first got married? You think that's what they thought their lives would become?"

"Maybe. You notice when they got married and when their first kid was born?"

"Good point."

He grabbed my hand and squeezed. "You know why I know we'd never be like that?"

"Why?"

"Because I'm not settling for you. You're exactly who I want to be with and who I love."

I squeezed back. "And you're exactly who I want to be with."

To change the subject before we got way too sappy, I said, "So. Looks like we're going to have an interesting interview with Rick tomorrow."

"That it does. He may have been the last one to see Julie alive."

CHAPTER SIXTEEN

W E   MET   R ICK   AT   THE   ACCOUNTING   FIRM   WHERE   HE
worked. It was located on the second floor of a three-story
office building tucked into the curve off Havana Street in
Aurora. The hallway carpet was a thin, faded beige and the
stairs we had to take to reach the second floor were narrow
and steep. But the offices themselves were nice enough.

Rick had clearly put on a few pounds and lost a few
inches of hairline since his picture on the website was taken.
He also seemed to have developed an inordinate fondness
for hair gel. It was not a good look.

But he still had attractive green eyes and good teeth. I
could see what Julie had found interesting about him all
those years ago.

He led us to a conference room with four gray fabric
chairs arranged around a black table. "Can I get you a
coffee? Tea?"

Matt took a coffee, but I waved him away and grabbed
the Coke I'd brought out of my purse. "Brought my own,
thanks."

That broke some of the tension in the room. He settled down across from us. "So? This is about that girl who got killed, huh? The one up in the mountains?"

Matt nodded. "The one you flirted with the night she died."

"Well, yeah. She was a good-looking girl, you know? She started talking to me, I started talking back. And then that friend of hers came and shoved in. Crazy guy. Threatened to call the cops just because we'd dropped in on his party. I took off. She was pretty, but not that pretty. And I had my own beer back at the cabin."

"That *crazy guy* says the girl followed you when you left the party."

Rick turned his coffee cup this way and that until it was perfectly aligned with the edge of the table, but he didn't answer.

"Did she?" Matt finally asked.

"Yeah."

"Why didn't you tell the cops?"

He grimaced. "I don't know. I didn't really want to get into it with them."

"Get into what?"

He scratched at his ear. "She followed me back to the cabin, right? My buddies had gone on to another party, so it was just us."

"Umhm. And?"

"And she was pretty." He shrugged as if what he was about to say was obvious. "So I made a few moves."

I tensed, but the coroner's report had said there was no sign of any sort of sexual contact, willing or otherwise.

"And?" Matt asked.

"And when I tried to take it past a little bit of kissing, she freaked out. Said she didn't want that. Pushed me away." He frowned like he couldn't understand why a woman might do such a thing.

"And then what happened?" Matt asked as I glared daggers at Rick and he pointedly avoided looking my direction.

"I said a few things. I don't like women who promise and don't deliver." He flicked me a glance but quickly looked away when I returned it with pure contempt. Such a class act. To know he was saying something rude, but not keep it to himself.

"And?" Matt asked again, a little more forcefully this time.

"She got all teary-eyed. Said I was mean. That she'd never promised me anything. I told her to go back to her little high school party, but she didn't want to. Said she didn't want to see that guy she'd gotten in a fight with. Asked if I could give her a ride home."

"What did you do then?" Matt asked, his voice carefully neutral, while I fumed silently.

"I said sure, why not. Figured she might warm up a bit if given the chance, you know?"

I tried very hard not to move. This was it. He was our murderer. He'd given her a ride home, she'd refused him again, and he'd killed her.

"And did you give her that ride?" Matt asked, closing the trap.

"No. Turns out Dave had left for some family emergency while I was gone. Which meant I didn't have a car to drive her home with."

I managed not to show my disappointment.

"So what happened then?"

He glanced my way. "She asked to use the phone in the cabin. Called some guy. He came and picked her up."

"She didn't go back to the party?"

"No. Just stayed and drank my beer until the guy got there. And the guy who picked her up? That guy would never have been invited to a party in high school. Short, glasses, acne, braces. He'd hit the trifecta of loserdom."

I valiantly refrained from pointing out how he'd listed four attributes, not three.

"Do you remember what kind of car he was driving?" Matt asked, glancing my way for a brief moment.

I made an effort to calm myself back down. I don't know how it works, but when I really, really don't like someone it's like I'm drilling a hole in their skull. The whole room seems to feel it even if I don't say a word. (Comes in handy when I need customer service to notice me, but incredibly awkward the rest of the time.)

Rick glanced my way again before he answered. "A station wagon with wood paneling. I remember I made fun of it. Suggested to her that she'd be better off staying with me than getting in that piece of junk, but she ignored me. Just begged the guy to get her out of there."

"Alright. Thank you." Matt stood, so I did, too.

Rick held the door for us, but I ignored him entirely. He may not have killed Julie but he was still a creep.

Matt and I were silent until we returned to the van. "Dennis Clay," I said. "That had to be who picked her up."

"You said he was hiding something."

"I didn't think it was murder." I backed out of the parking space with a little more speed than was probably safe.

"Well, only one way to find out. I'll have Ben bring him

in for a formal interview this afternoon. You can watch from observation."

I wanted to just drive by his house and confront him, but Matt was right. If he really was the killer, then the cops needed any confession he gave on tape and handled properly under the law.

That didn't mean I had to like it, though.

CHAPTER SEVENTEEN

WE WENT STRAIGHT TO THE POLICE STATION WHEN WE
reached Creek. They already had Dennis Clay in the interrogation room when we arrived. He was angry, I could see it
in the way he held the glass of water they'd given him, his
knuckles white from the tension.

It was further confirmed when he snapped at Matt as
soon as Matt entered the room. "When can I leave? I need
to get home to my mom. And I have work to finish today."

Matt sat down across from him with a casual grace. "I'm
sorry to bother you with this, Mr. Clay, but you understand
that the murder of a woman is serious business even if it
happened over a decade ago."

"So now the cops are investigating this, too? Not just
that woman who dropped by my house uninvited? What did
I say to her that you decided to haul me in here like a
common criminal?"

"Nothing. Although she did think you were hiding something." Matt paused long enough to give Dennis a mean-
ingful look. "It was the interview we conducted with Rick

Patterson today that led to you being brought in for questioning."

"Who is Rick Patterson?"

"Who do you think he is? Think back to the events surrounding Julie's death and tell me who might've pointed us in your direction."

Dennis's upper lip twitched as he glared at the corner of the room.

"Look, Mr. Clay, you can come straight with me about what you know about the death of Julie Lewis or I'll build my case without you. But your silence won't save you."

He stared at Matt, looking genuinely shocked. "Save me? I didn't hurt her."

"Then tell me what you know about the events surrounding her murder. And why you didn't come forward at the time."

He pushed away from the table and rubbed his hands on his jeans. "I didn't hurt her."

Matt spread his hands wide. "Okay. I'll believe you. For now. Are you willing to give a DNA sample?"

Dennis shifted in his seat. "I thought she wasn't...hurt... that way."

"She wasn't. But there have been incredible advances in DNA testing since she was murdered. We can tell if someone touched her. It's called touch DNA. Did you touch her, Dennis?"

"Not like that." He pressed his lips together and stared into the corner. "It wasn't like that."

"What was it like, Dennis? Tell me."

He fidgeted some more before finally answering. "She called me. It was late. She was clearly drunk. She was crying. She said she was down by the lake and needed a ride home. She asked me to come pick her up."

"Why you?"

"Because I lived nearby? Because she knew I'd be home? Because she knew I'd do anything for her? I don't know."

"So you picked her up."

"Of course I did. Julie Lewis called *me* to help her. What was I going to do? Say no."

"Did she tell you why she needed the ride?"

He shook his head. "Not really. She...She didn't want to talk. I tried, but she just huddled against the door and cried the whole way home. I asked her if that guy had done something to her and she shook her head, but that was all I could get out of her."

"You didn't like that, did you?" Matt snapped as he leaned forward. "You did something about it. Here you were, being the nice guy, picking her up from that stupid party, and she wouldn't even talk to you."

"What? No. It wasn't like that." He crossed his arms and hunched downward in his seat. "She was so sad. I didn't know what to say to her. I didn't know what to do. So I just drove her home."

"Is that all you did? You didn't pull over on the side of the road and try to get a little payment for the favor you were doing her?"

"No! Not at all. I'd never do that to Julie."

Matt leaned in even more. "Then why didn't you tell anyone about it when she was found dead the next morning? Didn't you want to help the police find her killer?"

He rubbed at his face. "I didn't think it mattered. She wasn't killed at home, right? And I knew if I told people that they'd react like you are. They'd accuse me of doing something to her. But I didn't do anything. I just picked her up and gave her a ride home. That's all."

"Can anyone confirm your story?"

He shook his head. "No. Her dad wasn't home when I dropped her off. My mom would've been able to tell you I got a call and was back by midnight, but she's in and out these days. I doubt she could remember one specific day like that. Not all these years later."

Matt stayed silent, watching Dennis until the tension in the air became almost unbearable.

Dennis shook his head. "I didn't kill her, I swear. I'll take a lie detector if you want."

"What about that DNA?"

"She was in my car. I squeezed her shoulder when she was crying. She may have my DNA on her. But not because I did anything to her."

Matt glanced towards where I stood watching the interview. "Anything else you can remember about that night?"

He shook his head. "She told me thank you when I dropped her off. Told me I was a true friend, someone she could always count on. She didn't say it, but there was an implication that someone else wasn't a true friend. And, no, I don't know who it would be."

"Did you see anyone else at the party?"

"I didn't see a party. I picked her up at some cabin. It was just her and some older guy. I don't even know where the party was supposed to be compared to that cabin, but it definitely wasn't anywhere within sight."

Matt nodded. "Okay. Stay in town. We may need to talk to you again."

I waited long enough for him to walk Dennis out the front door and then joined him at his desk. "So now what?"

"I don't know. We have a better timeline than the original investigators had. We know Julie made it home safe, assuming Dennis is telling the truth, and I think he is. But phone records don't show any calls to or from her house that night. So someone had to go to her house and pick her up. Or she had to leave to meet them. But who? And why?"

"That's the million-dollar question, isn't it? Who would come to Julie Lewis's house in the middle of the night instead of calling her? And who would she go off with at that time of night?"

"Exactly. Well, I better write up the interviews we did for the file. And then, dinner? Say six?"

I nodded. "I'm sure Lesley will have whipped up something interesting."

He caught my hand. "I prefer your cooking to hers, you know."

I laughed. "That's because you've never lived with me. Just know that sometimes I think that onion dip, chips, and a hunk of cheese is a perfectly acceptable dinner."

He grinned. "Sounds good to me. As long as you're occasionally okay with a can of tuna fish and some Doritos."

I gave him a kiss on the cheek and headed home, still trying to figure out what had drawn Julie Lewis away from her house in the middle of the night. (Assuming Dennis was telling the truth, of course.)

CHAPTER EIGHTEEN

Fancy practically bowled me over as soon as I opened the front door. I sat down so she could crawl all over me and lick my face until she finally calmed down. "It was only two nights, you goof," I told her.

But in dog-world I'm pretty sure any absence over an hour is a lifetime. She trailed after me as I put my bag away and stashed the leftover Coke in the kitchen pantry. (I still had six cans left, which considering that I'd put six in the cooler and started with two cases, was pretty good really.)

I checked the stove top which had a big batch of split pea soup cooking, and took a deep deep breath of the yummy smells coming from the bread maker. No signs of my grandpa or Lesley, so I figured they'd run somewhere real quick until dinner was ready. Never the best idea to leave food cooking on the stove without supervision, but they probably hadn't gone far or for long.

When I settled on the couch, Fancy jumped up next to me and stared at me, not lying down like she normally would. "I'm right here. I'm not going anywhere again anytime soon, okay?"

I couldn't imagine leaving Fancy for a month like Jamie and Mason had with Lulu when they went to Paris. I mean, Paris. But, Fancy. She hadn't asked me to take responsibility for her, I'd made that decision on my own. And since I had, I tried to do the best I could by her even if that meant no really good, lengthy vacations for a decade.

At loose ends and determined not to spend the time until dinner playing solitaire, I called Jamie.

"Maggie. How'd it go?"

"Well, we had some interesting interviews. I mean Barb Holt is…"

"I don't care about that. You're the only person I know who would combine interviewing people about a murder with your first getaway with your boyfriend. I'm sure that kept things interesting, but I want to know how your first weekend away with Matt went. Are you still together?"

"Yes, we're still together. Although he asked if I want kids." I shuddered.

"And what did you tell him?"

"That if I agreed to marry him I'd agree to try for kids, too."

"If? Maggie. Come on now. Who are you going to find that's more perfect for you than Matt?"

I pinched the bridge of my nose. "I don't know. Probably no one. But marriage is a big deal."

"Not really."

"How can you say that?"

"Look, Mason and I were great together before we got married and are even more great together now. Marriage didn't change anything."

"It's permanent and binding, Jamie. You have to like go to court if it doesn't work out."

She laughed. "Maggie, you are so crazy. Do you want to lose him?"

"No."

"Then marry him."

"He hasn't even asked." Fancy gave me a glare before jumping off the couch and going outside. She's not a fan of loud voices.

"And if he did, what would you say? Because you know darned well that if you give him the slightest indication that you're interested he'll ask."

I made some sort of noise that probably sounded like I was dying. "I don't know."

"He survived a weekend with you. In a van. For hours on end. Do you like him less now? Or more?"

"Probably more."

"Then marry him."

"He hasn't asked."

"He will. Soon. And when he does, you better say yes."

I rolled my eyes. "Just because you're happily married doesn't mean I will be."

"Maggie, you're never going to be perfectly happy. But you'll be much happier with Matt in your life than without him. I know you. Trust me. So say yes when he asks."

I narrowed my eyes, suddenly suspicious. "He hasn't talked to you about this, has he?"

"I am your best friend."

"What did you tell him, Jamie?" I snapped.

"I told him you were very skilled at avoiding discussions you didn't want to have. And that if he waited for you to give him the green light to ask he'd never get it. But that if he pushed the point and just went ahead and asked you that you'd almost certainly say yes."

"Jamie!"

"It's true."

I slumped down. "Doesn't mean you should've told him."

"Don't worry. You have until spring."

"Spring?"

"Better go. Mason just got home." She hung up.

When was spring? Months away, right? Like May?

I frantically searched for the first day of spring on my phone. Turns out it was in the middle of March. I had less than three weeks.

Matt was probably going to ask me to marry him in less than three weeks. No wonder he'd been talking about buying a place. And kids. For him this was right around the corner.

For a second, I forgot how to breathe. I wasn't ready for this. I needed…years. Decades, even. Centuries, really, but unfortunately the human life span didn't allow for that one.

I glanced at Fancy who had come back inside and gone to sleep at my feet, snuffling quietly to herself. I'd always wanted a dog, but had never found the time for one. And then Fancy came along. She had nowhere else to go— nowhere good at least—so I'd taken her on.

It had changed my life entirely. Probably for the good.

No. Definitely for the good.

I hated big commitments. They never made sense to me. They were so lasting and final. I'd taken Fancy on and for me that was a commitment to ten years of living my life differently, putting the needs of another living creature above my own. But it worked out okay, because she really couldn't tell me when I messed up and was easygoing enough to just roll with it.

But a human being would have opinions. And marriage was a commitment for the rest of my life not just ten years.

Jamie was right, though. If Matt asked I wouldn't be able to tell him no.

Fancy moved in her sleep and her paw stretched out to rest against my leg. I looked down at her for a long moment and sighed. As much as I didn't like to make them, big commitments were usually worth it.

CHAPTER NINETEEN

THE NEXT DAY I ASKED MR. LEWIS IF HE'D JOIN ME FOR lunch. We went to a BBQ joint in Masonville and I told him everything we'd found out about the night Julie died and then I apologized to him for not finding the killer.

"Don't be sorry. You found out more than the cops did back then. You really think Dennis Clay was telling the truth?"

I nodded. "I knew he was hiding something when I talked to him that first time. And after we talked to Rick Patterson, I thought maybe he was hiding the fact that he'd done something to Julie. But I just don't see it. Matt really grilled him and he held up."

I took a bite of my BBQ pork sandwich and managed to suppress my groan of pleasure. I don't eat BBQ often because even I know that too much fat is probably bad for your heart, but, man, that stuff is good. Especially the bits with the crispy fat...Mmmm.

"Had Julie ever snuck out of the house before that night that you knew of?" I asked.

"No."

"And why did she leave? Why not just let whoever it was into the house? She had to know you weren't going to be home for hours." I dipped my fries in the tangy barbecue sauce, relishing that mix of tartness and salt and starch. It was hard to focus on the conversation when the food was so good.

"That's easy enough to answer. My neighbor at the time, Ms. Franks, had horrible insomnia. She was up most of every night. And she took it upon herself to keep an eye on Julie. Every time Julie was up past midnight Ms. Franks would let me know. Not only that, she'd tell me which lights in the house were on and if there was a car in the driveway, what kind of car it was."

"Did that happen often?"

He shook his head. "Only a couple of times."

I forced myself to ignore my food for a few moments. This felt important. "And when there was someone over, who was it? Before that night, I mean."

"Tim. Always Tim."

"Not Barb and Tim?"

"No, just Tim. When Barb and Tim went anywhere together they always drove her SUV, because it was new and fancy. But Tim had access to an old pickup truck that had been his grandpa's. It wasn't really safe for the road, but he only lived a couple of miles away so it was safe enough to drive to our house and back."

"Did Ms. Franks see anything on the night Julie died?"

"I never asked her. I always assumed Julie didn't make it home."

"And she didn't tell you? She sounds like the type that would've immediately given you full details when she heard about Julie."

I snuck another fry dunked in barbecue sauce while he

rubbed at the back of his neck, thinking. "She had a stroke right around then. Might've been the same day they found Julie. I can't remember, I was so numb, so lost. They moved her into a home. She passed away a few months later."

I stored that fact away for later, but I had a more promising lead to explore first. "What about Amy Haverson? How close was Julie with her? There were some photos in the yearbook and one or two mentions in her diary, but that's about it."

He shook his head. "They were never really close. I mean, same age, grow up in the same small town, you don't tend to have a lot of choices about your friends. But Amy was always a little on the wild side. She was always testing to see where the lines were. Led her to make some bad choices. Julie stayed away from that."

"That fits with what I know of her. Amy overdosed five years ago."

"I know. Her dad and I were friends. She was headed that way from a very young age."

"I was kind of hoping she'd had some involvement in Julie's murder and spiraled from there." I took another bite of my sandwich. It wasn't as good when it wasn't hot.

He shook his head. "I don't think so. But her dad still has all of her things. You want me to give him a call? Maybe she had a diary like Julie did."

"It's worth a shot."

Believe it or not, we spent the rest of the meal talking about the television show *Chopped*. It turns out we were both fans and they'd just had a barbecue special episode we'd both watched. Discussing that episode led to a long discussion about other episodes we'd watched. My personal favorite was the April Fool's episode with the caramel-covered onion. I'd liked all the misdirects with foods that weren't what they seemed. His favorites were the teen competitions because it reminded him of what amazing potential kids have.

It was a nice meal overall. And good to see him share a meal rather than eat alone and stare out the window at nothing for once. I promised myself I'd try to make a habit of it after the investigation was over. It was good for both of us, really.

———

Turns out Amy did have a diary. Or a journal of sorts. Actually three of them. They were more pictures than words. Lots of dark, angry, black drawings of tortured faces and dripping blood. It was hard to reconcile those images with the relatively clean-cut yearbook photos I'd seen.

I asked her dad about it. He was a short man whose large belly pushed against the seams of the white shirt he'd tucked into a pair of old jeans.

"She wanted to dye her hair black junior year of high school. I told her if she did I'd send her off to live with her aunt who was a former Marine. Same with when she tried to wear ripped jeans and black t-shirts with violent images on them. The threat worked until she turned eighteen that June."

"Did she stay around here after that?" I glanced around the small, cramped living room. There wasn't a single sign in that room that he'd ever had a daughter.

"Nope. She blew out the birthday candles on her cake, walked out the front door, and hitched the first ride she could find." He glanced out the window to where we could see the interstate running by half a block away.

"How'd she react to Julie's death?"

He shrugged. "I think she wished it was her. She had this idea that she was destined to die young. Said she couldn't believe goody-goody Julie had beat her to it. But other than that, it was like it didn't happen."

"Did she hang around with anyone that summer?"

"Not really. Not that I saw. No one came by. I know she went out to the lake to party like the other kids, but other than that she wasn't close to anyone." He scratched at his belly. "I tried to talk to her. I did. I worried so much about her, but..." He shrugged. "I wasn't very good at it. I got impatient. And angry. And then she'd leave. And that was that."

"Have you read these?" I put my hand on the journals he'd dug out of the closet.

"From time to time. She used to leave them lying around the house. But I didn't like what I saw, so I stopped."

I wondered if that had been her way of trying to communicate with her father. Not every kid can talk to their parents, after all. "Well, thank you for letting me borrow them. I really appreciate it."

"Keep 'em. Not doing me any good anymore."

"Oh, no, I wouldn't want to do that. You never know when you might change your mind."

He nodded, but it was clear he wanted them gone for good. I quickly made my excuses and got out of there.

CHAPTER TWENTY

EXPLORING THOSE JOURNALS WAS FASCINATING AND disturbing at the same time. When I'd read Julie's diary it had felt familiar. We'd grown up in different places and under different circumstances, but we were a lot alike. High achievers comfortable in our own skin and our belief that life was going to work out.

But Amy's journals were an insight into a type of worldview I'd never experienced and honestly struggled to understand. Not a worldview in the sense of what she thought of other people or her religious or social beliefs, but in terms of how she approached the world and what happened in it.

It was mostly drawings, but those drawings combined with the few words she used were all about the darkness in life, about failure and loss and inevitable decay. About not feeling comfortable with who she was and who the world wanted her to be.

A part of me wanted to believe that she was the killer, because then there'd be some logic or explanation for what I saw on those pages. Some inner corruption that was reflected outwardly in what she did. But after reading all three journals I knew she wasn't the killer.

She was just a sad, lonely girl struggling with depression and with a parent who didn't understand the bleakness that filled her soul, and so couldn't give her the help that might have saved her from the path she'd gone down.

I set the journals aside and went to find Fancy to snuggle with for a few minutes. Of course, Fancy isn't a snuggler so as soon as I sat close enough to her that she thought I was going to actually intrude on her space she got up and moved to the other side of the room with a look like, "What is wrong with you person? Boundaries, please."

"Everything alright?" my grandpa asked, coming into the room.

"No." I told him about the journals and about how sad it made me to think how many people walk through the world with that kind of inner darkness eating away at them. I finished with, "From what I could tell, she had a decent enough life, Grandpa. But she was so…angry and sad and confused."

"You can never know what someone else is carrying around inside. And you can never understand how much that life that seemed good to you wasn't for her. I can't tell you how many times I've seen it with the kids I've coached over the years. For the ones who fit into the lines that their parents draw for them, life is easy. It's charmed. But every few years I get a kid through who seems like they should have it all worked out and they're drowning. Because who they are inside doesn't match what the world they live in wants them to be." He nodded towards the door. "Jack, Matt's brother, was one of those. He had the looks and the brains and the charm to be anything he wanted to be. But he messed up all the time, because his dad wanted him to be something he couldn't be."

(Jack was quite the gentleman criminal before he finally decided to turn it around.)

"Matt turned out fine, though," I said.

"Yes and no. Matt struggled, too. Don't think he didn't. But he found a way out—the military. If he hadn't found that path, I don't know where he would've ended up."

It's hard to realize that someone you love could actually have turned out completely different given just a few different choices along the way. But it's true. Our choices drive us down certain paths but then those paths turn right back around and shape us into the people we become. Which is why the paths we choose are so important.

Like marriage. Twining your life so closely with anyone else is bound to change everything from that moment forward.

"Grandpa."

"Yeah?"

"Do you think I should marry Matt?"

He shook his head. "That's your choice to make. But please make it soon before you drive all of us crazy. As they say, it's time to put up or shut up."

Fancy rolled onto her side with a loud grunt as if agreeing with him.

I glanced at those journals again. Who did I want to be? The person who saw darkness and despair down every possible path? Or the one (like Jamie) who saw it all as one great, wonderful adventure that was bound to work out one way or the other?

I'd always had faith in my ability to accomplish things. Jump out of a plane and land in one piece, no problem. Quit my job, move halfway across the country, and open a business not many people would find interesting, done. Get an MBA, sure. Get a promotion, absolutely.

But people always stymied me. They were these fathomless black holes that I could throw my love or interest or attention at, but what happened after that was a great, vast mystery I didn't really understand or trust.

I trusted Matt, though. To my core. Which meant, it seemed, that I was going to have to get married.

Damn it. (Sorry for the language, but, really, a moment like that called for it.)

CHAPTER TWENTY-ONE

I WANTED TO SOLVE JULIE'S MURDER FIRST, THOUGH. Which meant actually figuring out who had lured Julie away from her house that night.

I sat down with a piece of paper and started writing down names.

Hank. A violent drunk. Definitely capable of hurting her. But I couldn't see Julie leaving her house with him. They weren't especially close. Plus, he'd probably just passed out at the party. He'd be a suspect if she'd died there and not near her house, but she hadn't. So he was out.

Amy. A sad, depressed teenager with dark thoughts. It wasn't outside the realm of possibility that she'd want to hurt someone else, but there'd been an entry in her journal from the night of the party, and I didn't see her writing that entry and then leaving her house to go kill Julie.

Dennis Clay. Another probably sad and depressed teenager. He did have that restraining order from college, but he hadn't tried to hurt that girl in college, he'd just been uncomfortably attentive. And I couldn't see him hurting

Julie. Pining after her? Sure. Making her uncomfortable with his awkward attempts to get to know her? Absolutely. (Been on the receiving end of that once or twice, myself.) But I believed him when he said he'd driven her home that night and then left.

Rick (the you-know-what). Hadn't had access to a car. And if he'd been going to do something I'm pretty sure it would've been before driving her home, not after. He didn't even know where she lived either, come to think of it.

Tim and Barb. I didn't know. Maybe. But why was I thinking of them as a unit? Because Lesley said they were always joined at the hip? Or because they were still together?

I realized I shouldn't be thinking of them that way. I should be thinking of them as two very different people with very different needs.

Tim. Had told Julie he loved her and she'd walked away. I could see him going to her house that night and trying to make it right. Trying to get back that friendship they'd shared all those years. Or to make his case again.

But would he then kill her? For what? For rejecting him? That's definitely the danger point in most abusive relationships, the point where the woman tries to leave. But they'd just been friends. Would he really kill her like that? And there were no signs he was an abuser either.

He was strong enough to do it, though. And he was certainly one of the people Julie would probably leave her house for.

Which meant he had to stay on the list. He was my strongest possibility so far.

Barb. She'd heard Tim confess his love to Julie. She knew she was his second choice. And that he was willing to give her up for Julie if Julie said yes. Had she lured Julie out of her house so she could take care of her competition for good?

But would Julie leave her house in the middle of the night for Barb? They were friends, but were they that close?

(Me, I'd only leave the house if someone was in a dire emergency that required immediate action. Otherwise I'd be like, "Why are you at my door? Do you not understand that it's the middle of the frickin' night? Go away and come back at a decent hour." But I'm also anti-social and rude.)

I tried to put myself in Julie's shoes. She'd gone to her first party. She was drunk for the first time. She'd flirted with some guy who turned out to be a jerk. Her best friend of forever had confessed he was in love with her. She'd had to call the guy she probably knew was in love with her but that she wasn't interested in for a ride home. And now she was home, all alone.

That summer was supposed to be this great, wonderful adventure where she got to let loose a little after so much drive and passion, but the first night had been an absolute disaster. Who could she talk to about that? Not her dad. He was at work. So a friend? But which one?

Barb?

I could see her agreeing to go off somewhere with Barb to talk it through except for the Tim situation. That was awkward. But if she confessed to Barb that she didn't want Tim, would that make it doable?

Maybe.

We knew Barb and Tim had left the party and gone back to Tim's house together. But what if they didn't stay together? Then it could've been either one of them.

Or what if they had? What if Barb had turned on Tim

that night and they'd had a huge fight and she'd said that if he really loved her he needed to take care of Julie. That she was coming between them. That if he really cared about her, he'd help her do something about it for once and for all. Would he do that for Barb?

Did they have that dynamic?

I wasn't so sure.

Then again, they were clearly miserable in their lives, but still together. *Something* was holding them there. But what? Mutual guilt over the murder of Julie?

Of course, people stay in awful relationships for any number of reasons, and 99.99% of the time it's not because they killed someone together.

For Barb it could be thinking she'd won the prize and now being stuck with Tim even though it turned out all he could offer her was an average life in a small town.

For Tim it could be about duty. Or religious belief. (I hadn't seen signs of religious belief in their house, though.) Or it could be figuring there was nothing better out there or staying for the kids.

(The worst reason to stay in a relationship ever from my observations.)

So maybe their misery had nothing to do with Julie's murder.

I didn't know. And I didn't know how to find out.

What I did know is that I needed some fresh air.

I grabbed Fancy's leash. In less than two seconds she went from a snoring, slobbering mess to wide awake and on her feet, staring at the door. (Must be some doggie survival trick, because I certainly can't pull that off.)

"I take it you're up for a walk then?" I asked as she came over to let me leash her up.

As we stepped outside, I cursed under my breath. How

had I forgotten that it was winter in the mountains of Colorado, which meant it was *cold*? (I try not to go for walks when I can literally see my breath.) Ah well. Too late to go back once a hundred and forty pounds of eager dog started pulling me down the street.

CHAPTER TWENTY-TWO

THAT NIGHT MATT CAME OVER FOR DINNER AND I TALKED through my suspect list with him and my grandpa. Lesley was at her youngest grandkid's school pageant and my grandpa had managed to excuse himself. I didn't blame him. There's a point where kids move from adorably incompetent to just horrendous sounding and little Bobby was at that age. The only people who were going to enjoy that particular performance were besotted parents or grandparents.

Since Lesley wasn't there I'd made dinner. Spaghetti casserole. There's just something about massive amounts of Velveeta melted over noodles, spaghetti sauce, and spicy sausage that really works well together. Pair it with some nice crunchy French bread and real butter and it's a winning combination.

(Then again, any meal that involves cheese is already halfway to delicious in my book with the exception of gorgonzola which I swear is a sign that evil lurks in the corners of the world. I will never forgive those gorgonzola mashed potatoes that absolutely ruined a nice, juicy steak for me back when I was basically living on room service meals.)

As I judiciously fed Fancy small bites of cheese and noodles—I didn't think she needed spicy sausage—I asked Matt if he could maybe call Tim and ask him if he and Barb had spent that entire night together. "At least then we'd know whether to look at them as a couple or on their own."

"I'd rather not if we can avoid it."

I must've frowned at him, because he chuckled a bit and added, "If I'm going to go back to them for another interview I want more information and I want them in an interview room."

"You can't possibly think of bringing them here with five kids in tow."

"I will if I think they're murderers." He stabbed a piece of sausage with his fork. "But we need a lot more to go on before we make that decision. There was nothing in Amy's journals?"

"No. She wasn't much for words. And it's hard to know which of the drawings were real events and which were fantasies. There were some pretty disturbing drawings in there. Lots of Barb and Julie and a few others. For example…"

I ran over and grabbed the most recent journal and flipped through to show them one of the sketches. "See, here's Barb and her face is all twisted up in a snarl. And here's Julie with her head down reading a book. And then here's Amy on her knees, crying. But they're all separate images. See that? They're on the same page, but there's no way to know if they were drawn at the same time or if they're supposed to be connected."

My grandpa flipped through the sketches, raising his eyebrows at what he saw. "Is there any pattern?"

"Maybe. Barb is usually looking mean when she's drawn. Julie is usually daydreaming or disconnected from what's happening. A few of the other girls look mean sometimes, too. And Amy generally looks angry or hurt. Which pretty much confirms what I already knew about Barb, which is that she's a, you know. And that Julie was off studying and playing sports most of the time."

My grandpa showed me a drawing. "Tim?"

"Yeah, probably."

Matt took the journal from my grandpa and showed the page to both of us. "Look at who he's watching."

I nodded. "Julie. But then that also confirms what we already knew. One big ol' love triangle that Julie was oblivious to. Do you kill over that? If you're Barb? Or if you're Tim and the girl you love rejects you?"

My grandpa took the list of suspects and glanced at it. "You left off one possibility."

"What's that?"

"A stranger."

"But she was half a mile from her house. Do you really think she walked half a mile in the middle of the night by herself and then just happened to stumble upon someone who decided to kill her but not do anything else?"

He shrugged and handed it back. "It's still a possibility."

I tossed the journal and list aside in disgust. "I wish that busybody, Ms. Franks, was still alive. Mr. Lewis said she knew which cars came by, license plate and all. Someone like that, she probably kept a written record of it. But Mr. Lewis said she had a stroke right after Julie died."

"Hm." My grandpa reached for his non-existent cigarettes and then frowned when he remembered he no longer smoked. "It's a long shot, but her son is a bit of a hoarder. It's possible he actually kept his mother's things."

"It's been over ten years."

"What would that matter to a hoarder? Of course, if it turns out he did keep a notebook of hers that says who came by that night, that will make him even worse than he is now."

I shuddered, thinking about the few episodes of that show on hoarders that I'd watched. Give me an episode of *Intervention* any day, but *Hoarders*? Ugh. No. I draw my line at...ugh. I won't even say it. Just, no.

"Maybe we don't have to tell him if we find something," I said.

"Good luck with that."

I glanced at Matt. "Are you up for it? Swinging by his place tomorrow to see what he kept?"

He nodded. "Sure. I'd like to see this solved as much as you would at this point. Even if it means wading through piles of old newspapers."

"And worse. Don't forget the worse." I shuddered.

CHAPTER TWENTY-THREE

THE NEXT DAY WE DROVE OUT TO BEAU FRANKS'S HOUSE. It was a one-story house on the edge of town. It looked weary but not neglected. The paint was fresh enough, the window screens were well-repaired. But there was a sag to the house that made me feel like it might collapse in a puff of dust any day.

Matt banged on the door. He was in his uniform. (Which looked mighty nice on him, I might add.) This was a quasi-official visit. His boss had kind of sort of signed off on my participation in the police investigation. (Mostly because he knew not signing off wouldn't change my involvement and at least this way he looked like he was in control of the situation.)

Beau, when he finally opened the door, was much like his house. His clothes were clean enough. He didn't smell or anything like that. But he looked worn and on the point of collapse. A cat wove its way between his legs before shooting outside after prey only it could see. The odor wafting through the door was decidedly musky, but not rotten like I'd feared it would be.

"Beau Franks?" Matt asked.

"That's me."

"Officer Barnes. And this is Maggie Carver. We'd like to ask you a few questions if you don't mind."

Beau angled his hip against the doorframe, clearly blocking us from coming into the house. It was not a warm enough day to be having any sort of lengthy conversation on the front step, so I added, "We can do it in the police SUV if you'd rather we didn't come inside."

He glanced towards the SUV. "That thing have prisoner locks?"

Matt answered. "It does."

I added, "But I can sit in the back if you'd like. You can sit up front with Matt."

He raised his eyebrows in surprise. "Understand that I'd like to invite you in, that's how my mama raised me. But it's not fit for company in here. I haven't cleaned up in a while."

"Understood," Matt said, with a casual smile.

Beau glanced at the SUV one more time. "What's this about?"

"The murder of Julie Lewis. She was a neighbor of your mother's. We think your mother may have kept a record of who she saw at her neighbors' houses and that this could help us figure out who killed Julie."

He nodded. "No need to go to your SUV for that. She did keep records. Come on." He slipped on a pair of snow boots that were sitting by the door and led us towards a large shed perched near the side of the house. We had to truck through about six inches of snow to get to it. Clearly it wasn't a place he went to often.

He pulled a string of keys out of his pocket and unlocked the small padlock on the door. The hinges creaked as he pulled the right-hand door open, pushing snow out of the way a few inches at a time until there was room to see inside.

It smelled...stale. No mildew or rot or decay, just...stale. Like the air hadn't moved in a century or two.

"This is all my mama's stuff. I never had the chance to go through it, but didn't want to get rid of it neither."

"Any idea where the record we're looking for might be?" I asked looking at the boxes piled all the way to the ceiling, at least two deep along the walls.

"Nope. But the boxes are labeled. See? *Kitchen. Bedroom.*"

Matt nodded to him. "Do you mind if we take some of these boxes with us to look through?"

"You'll bring them back when you're finished?"

"Yes, we will. Any particular room you think is most likely?"

He thought about it for a minute, his face completely blank. "Kitchen or Bedroom, probably. Could also be the Living Room."

Well, that narrowed it down, didn't it? At least we could skip the bathroom boxes.

Beau rubbed at his arms. "Well, I'll leave you to it. Lock up when you leave if you don't mind."

He trudged back to the house. Matt took a gingerly step into the shed.

"Are you sure you want to do that?" I asked.

"Seems sturdy enough."

"I'll take your word for it." I stayed outside, shivering.

"It's also warmer in here."

"I'll still take your word for it."

He laughed. "So. Where do you think we can set up these boxes?"

"I would say my grandpa's house, but not knowing what might be lurking inside those boxes, there's no way I'm bringing them anywhere near where I have to sleep. So maybe...the community center in Creek?"

The community center was a large single-room brick building that was always too cold, but did have a nice assortment of long folding tables and uncomfortable chairs to go along with them. It didn't get much use in the winter months since the furnace that was supposed to heat it was usually on the fritz.

"Good idea. Let me make some calls."

CHAPTER TWENTY-FOUR

MATT MADE HIS CALLS WHILE WE WARMED OURSELVES UP in the SUV. It only took about ten minutes for him to confirm that no one was using the community center, to arrange to use it for the next week, and to get permission from his boss for the whole operation. We had to wait another ten minutes for someone to run us over the official crime scene camera so we could document the location of the boxes before we moved them.

As we sat in the SUV with the heaters blowing at full blast making my skin so warm it almost gave me shivers, I said, "You know. I think at this point this is definitely a police operation, which means you really don't want some untrained person like me handling those boxes."

Matt leveled a gaze my way. "You're not getting out of this that easy, Maggie May."

"Who said I was trying to get out of this? I'm just worried about the integrity of the investigation. This is physical evidence we're talking about."

"And I'd maybe believe you if you hadn't already handled both Julie and Amy's diaries. But since you did, I suspect this has far more to do with spiders than evidential procedure."

"Not just spiders. I'm also not too thrilled about running across any of those squirmy little bugs with too many legs and pincher mouths. And mice. And mice droppings. And who knows what else. Have you ever watched that hoarder show? Ew."

"Don't you want to catch a murderer?"

"Absolutely. And I have no doubt that you and whoever helps you will find the record you need to do so. Don't *you* want to catch the murderer?"

"I do. Which is why I will be sitting in that freezing-cold community center, wearing plastic gloves that make my palms itch, sorting through the effects of a woman who has been dead over a decade. But I'm not doing it alone. You got me into this, you're staying in it."

I shook my head. "See, this is the kind of crap you get yourself into when you decide for better or for worse. Moldy boxes in freezing concrete buildings."

"When you decide for better or for worse?" Matt grinned at me.

I held up a finger. "After we find the killer. And not until spring. But, yeah. If you ask, I'll say yes. I would've just set the whole thing up and sprung it on you, but I know you're the traditional type so you'll want to ask and make it all official. Let me just tell you now, I don't pretty cry, so prepare yourself."

He leaned back against the door, a big grin on his face. "Alright. I will. And what did you mean set the whole thing up and spring it on you?"

"Something like this is best handled like a Band-Aid. Just get it over with. You ask, I say yes, we do it, done. The less delay and anticipation, the better. You know I actually had a friend who was engaged for two and a half years? Her engagement lasted longer than the marriage. Crazy. Seriously, I do not need one special day of my life taking up that much mental space."

"So just get it over with, huh?"

"Yes."

"As soon as possible?"

"Yes."

I didn't think it was possible, but he grinned even more than he had been before. "Alrighty, then. But it's not getting you out of helping me with these boxes. I love you, but I don't love you that much."

"Haha. Funny." I glanced in the rearview. "Maybe we can get Officer Clark to do all the work."

"Not likely. Come on. Let's lock and load."

CHAPTER TWENTY-FIVE

Officer Clark did help us load the boxes into the back of Matt's SUV and his own. The whole time I kept waiting for a spider to crawl on my hand or for the bottom of a box to be suspiciously damp. But maybe because everything had been stored in a shed that was often below freezing for over a decade, we didn't run into a single bug or mouse. It was amazing. It gave me hope that the task wouldn't be all that horrible.

But once we unloaded the boxes at the community center that was the end of Officer Clark's involvement. He said he had to go man a speed trap outside of Bakerstown. I suspected he was making it up, but Matt wasn't going to stop him when that was where he was headed.

Which left Matt and me standing in the middle of the community center surrounded by ninety-two boxes of old lady belongings.

(My apologies if you're an old lady yourself, it's not meant to be an insult. It's just that older people acquire some strange belongings, especially those who lived through the Great Depression. There was half a box of neatly-folded wrapping paper that had clearly been saved from prior packages for reuse. I could appreciate the desire not to waste something like that while at the same time really wishing she'd been much younger and much less interested in holding onto anything that wasn't absolutely necessary.)

There was also an entire container of pens that were almost all dried out. (In a perverse moment of boredom, I uncapped a number of them and tried them on a notepad that only had three sheets left. I didn't think Beau would miss it.

"Maggie..." Matt said, from across the room where he was sorting through a box that seemed to be mostly plastic coat hangers. "These are still her belongings."

"Do you honestly think her son, after more than ten years, is going to miss a notepad from the Quality Inn that has three pages left on it?"

"No. But it's the principle of the thing. Plus, the sooner we find where she recorded the activities of her neighbors, the sooner we can be done with this. And get on to better things." He grinned at me again and I knew he was thinking about our wedding.

Why had I told him about that? What was I thinking? Now I couldn't back out.

I returned to my set of boxes with a renewed effort, more to channel my nervous energy than because I wanted to speed things along faster than they were already going.

As much as we tried to hurry, it still took a lot of time. Matt insisted that we photograph the exterior and interior of every box we opened, assign each one a number, and then create an inventory list of what was in the box. I saw the point in doing so, but it was still tedious.

On my tenth box I finally found one of Ms. Franks's day

planners. It was one of those big ones that have two pages devoted to each and every day. The ones she preferred didn't have the times listed already, they just had the day of the month and a bunch of skinny lines. She wrote in the time of day herself and then a bunch of illegible scrawls next to that.

"Matt."

"What?"

"Is this shorthand?" I still hadn't bothered to learn it myself, but I remembered very well that he knew how to use it. I hate being at a disadvantage like that.

He took the day planner from my hand. "It is."

"What does it say?"

"7:15 JL left house. Wearing blue coat. 7:20 Bus picked up JL. 8:25 CL left house. Black shirt, no coat." He flipped through the pages, scanning each one quickly. "And that's pretty much what it says for each and every day. Different coats or different times, but it looks like she noted down when the five or six people who lived within view of her house arrived or left, every, single day."

"That's it?"

"Oh, there are also notes about the mailman in here. And it seems one of her neighbors had a new couch delivered at one point. There are also some notes about the weather, but only on days when it rained or snowed from what I can see."

"Any opinions? Thoughts? Feelings?"

He shook his head. "Nope. Just facts. She would've made a good investigator, actually." He glanced at the cover. "Too bad this is the wrong year."

I pointed to the box I'd pulled the planner from. "Not the only one, I'm afraid. I'll double-check, but I suspect that since this box came from the bedroom that these are the ones she'd already filled in. But this is what we're looking for. At least we now know they exist."

Matt went back to his boxes, whistling happily to himself. I mentally grumbled as I quickly scanned the rest of the day planners in the box. A decade of monitoring every little detail of her neighbors' lives, but not the one day I needed.

Figured.

CHAPTER TWENTY-SIX

IT TOOK ANOTHER HOUR AND AN ENCOUNTER WITH ONE very ugly spider for me to finally find the day planner I needed. It was buried at the bottom of a box that included a set of twelve paper-towel-wrapped glasses, a roll of duct tape, two pairs of scissors, three baggies worth of rubber bands, a spool of twine, two screwdrivers, and a hammer.

(Someone really hadn't put much thought into their packing. The fact that those glasses survived that hammer was amazing. They almost didn't survive my excited squee and reach when I saw the corner of the day planner at the very bottom of the box and started to pull it out without removing everything else first.)

Matt was at my side almost instantly, helping me to carefully remove all twelve glasses before I pulled the day planner free. I immediately handed it to him.

"So?" I asked, practically dancing in place as he flipped through the pages.

"Give me a minute to get to the right page."

I peered over the edge of the day planner as he continued to flip through. I knew I shouldn't have given it to him until I found the page we needed. Never give a slow driver something that you need done in a hurry.

"Maggie."

"I want to see."

"Found it." He turned so we could both see the relevant pages.

We scanned the entries. There was Julie leaving for the party. There was Julie coming home from the party. Both included the make and model of the vehicle and the license plate.

But that was the last entry. Dennis Clay bringing Julie home.

I cussed. "I thought we had it." I leaned against the table just long enough to realize that was a very bad idea.

"Maybe..." Matt turned the page and I jumped back up. "Ha! Look."

He pointed at an entry right at the top of the page. 3:20 in the morning. Make, model, and license plate for the vehicle that picked her up.

"That's it. We have them." I made Matt flip back a page. "So it was Barb. Or Barb and Tim. Right?"

"Looks like it. Definitely the same vehicle and they did admit to picking her up and taking her to the party."

"We got 'em!" I did a little hip shake dance around the room, singing the words a few more times. "We got 'em, we got 'em."

"Maggie. Not so fast."

"What do you mean?"

"This is still just circumstantial evidence. A woman who is dead and can't testify about what she saw wrote something in a day planner over a decade ago. I doubt they'll even be able to use this if it comes to a trial."

"But they did it."

"Just because one of them—and we don't even know for sure which one or even if it was Barb or Tim—killed her, we don't know which one. We don't know how, we don't know why. It's not going to be enough to bring a case against them. If we don't get a confession, we won't be able to close this case."

I cussed. "They killed a young girl who had her whole life before her. They deserve to pay, Matt."

"But which one? Maybe it was an accident."

"An accident? She was struck three times. That's not an accident."

"Some people lose it in the moment. They don't even know what they're doing."

I crossed my arms and glared at him. "Murder is murder."

He set the day planner on the table. "If only it were that simple."

"But it is. One or both of them picked up Julie Lewis at three in the morning, drove her to that pullout off the highway, and attacked her. People don't go around carrying large dangerous objects in their hands. Whoever did this had to deliberately grab whatever they used when they talked to Julie."

"I don't disagree with you, Maggie. I'm just saying that we won't really know what happened until whoever did this tells us. Until then it's just a guess. And a guess isn't going to get us a conviction."

I thought about it. Darn it, he was right. "So we need to bring them in for questioning."

"They live in Kansas. And have five children. We can't bring them in that easy. We need more."

I paced the room, thinking. "Barb's family moved away, right?"

He nodded.

"But Tim's mom is still around. We could try her."

"Maybe."

"And the vehicle. They don't still own it, I don't think. Maybe they sold it to someone around here."

"Julie wasn't killed in the vehicle. She was killed on the side of the road."

"But whatever was used to hit her, wasn't left there. It was in the vehicle. After. And...Well."

He nodded. "And there could be DNA."

"Maybe. Long shot. Especially if it's been used by someone all these years."

"It's still worth a try. Let me see what I can find out tomorrow at work. And then we'll put together a game plan. But, Maggie?" He took hold of my shoulders and held my gaze.

"Yes?"

"You can't tell anyone what we found. Not yet. Especially not Mr. Lewis."

"He deserves to know, Matt."

"And he will. When we have something concrete to tell him."

I pulled away and paced the room again. "What if we never do? What if this is as close as we get to finding the killer?"

"Then we tell him we tried and we couldn't find the killer. We do not tell him about the entry in this day planner or the vehicle it identified."

"Why?"

"Because what do you think he'd do?"

I stopped and crossed my arms, pouting. "Confront them."

"Exactly. Imagine that. Poor Mr. Lewis driving to

Kansas, banging down their door, accusing them of killing his daughter, and likely getting arrested for it. That man does not deserve jail time after everything else he's been through."

I pressed my lips together and glared. "Then we damn well better find the killer. Or else I'll be the one driving to Kansas to confront those two."

Matt kissed my forehead. "We'll do what we can. And if that includes my taking your car keys away until you calm down, I'll do that, too. Can't have my future wife going to jail now can I?"

I shuddered at that word—wife. Ugh. The things we do for love...

CHAPTER TWENTY-SEVEN

MATT DID SOME DIGGING AROUND THE NEXT DAY. IT turned out that Barb's parents had given her a brand-new car for her birthday that fall and she'd given the SUV to Tim's mom who hadn't had a reliable vehicle up until that point. His mom was still driving it. Which meant that if we inspected the vehicle, we'd be giving away a key piece of information to our suspects.

(Look at me, saying "we" as if I was any part of that conversation whatsoever. Matt was still keeping me in the loop, but things had developed to the point where it was his job to bring everything home and I was just a cheerleader on the sidelines.)

It took about a week, but they finally arranged for Matt to re-interview both Barb and Tim at the police station in Salina. No way they were going to get permission to bring them back to Creek, not without a confession.

Since I had absolutely nothing going on in my life, I went with him. Our *second* long car trip together. This one with a small little snowstorm that left somewhere between an inch and three inches of snow on the road. I, ironically, seem to do better in severe weather driving than in good weather because I know I have to maintain focus. (Most of my early car accidents involved some form of "ooh, isn't that interesting" distractions while someone ahead of me stopped unexpectedly.)

Matt, on the other hand, kinda crumbled when it snowed. He was already a slow driver, but Matt and snow? A turtle could've driven faster. So after about ten miles of that, I made him switch with me even though we were in Kansas and it meant I might get a ticket. I figured better a speeding ticket than strangling my boyfriend to death for driving so slow he might as well be in reverse.

We made it. (Eventually.)

Matt decided to interview Tim first, figuring that he hadn't been involved that night and would quickly turn on Barb. Or, on the off chance he had been involved, that he was the most likely to feel incredibly guilty and break.

The station didn't have a separate room to stand in and observe like we had in Creek. But there was a recording room where the action played out live on a computer monitor. The officer who was assisting Matt didn't really want to let me watch, but Matt took him aside and convinced him to do it anyway.

Tim didn't look nervous at all. At least no more than the average person would when brought into a police station for questioning. As he waited for Matt he played some game on his phone that involved swiping things around.

But when Matt stormed into the room, Tim immediately dropped the phone in his lap and sat up straight.

Matt threw his folder down. "Were you there?"

"Where?" Tim shook his head, clearly bewildered.

"There when she was killed?"

(We'd had the officer advise Tim of his rights before

Matt entered the room so that Matt could be a little bit of a drama queen right off the bat.)

"Who? Julie? No. I told you I don't know who killed her! Don't you think I'd tell you guys if I did? I loved Julie. She was my everything." Tim looked genuinely surprised by the accusation.

"So what does that make Barb?" Matt asked.

Tim let out a deep sigh and slumped in his seat. "My wife."

"Aren't you supposed to marry the woman who's your everything?" Matt said it with just enough of a sneer that even I felt offended by his tone.

Tim put his phone on the table like a man going to his execution. "I would've. I loved Julie."

Matt crossed his arms and glared down at Tim. "Did you? Seems you were quick enough to pick up with Barb when she came around."

"It was…I didn't realize…I mean I'd always loved Julie since we were little. But I didn't realize it was that kind of love until…it was too late." He spun his phone in little circles on the table, not looking at Matt.

"Too late? You told her you loved her that night."

"And it all went wrong. She didn't want me."

"Do you blame her? She'd spent the last year or more watching some other girl hang off your arm every minute of every day and then you suddenly tell her you love her? What did you expect her to do?"

Tim buried his face in his hands. "I know. I screwed up. I never thought it was a possibility, you know?" He threw himself back in his chair. "I thought she was gonna go away to college and meet some guy who had everything. But then at that party she started talking to that jerk loser and I realized *I* was better than *that*. That if she'd go for him, she'd certainly go for me."

"So you tried."

"Yeah."

Matt slammed the table. "And she turned you down. Told you she didn't want you."

Tim rubbed his hands through his hair. "It wasn't like that. She was drunk and she was mad at me for chasing that guy off. For always being around but never being the guy who wanted to be with her. And when I told her I did want to be with her, then she just got even more mad because I'd waited so long to tell her and what were we supposed to do now. Barb was her friend."

He slumped even further in his chair.

Matt waited him out.

"And then she left. I think..." Tim pressed his lips together. "I think looking back at it now, that we could've worked it out when she sobered up. She'd think about it and we'd talk about it and we could be together. I actually woke up the next morning hoping that's what would happen."

"But that's not what you thought in the moment, was it? Not as she was walking away from you to go after that jerk loser, as you put it."

He buried his face in his hands. "No. I thought it was over. I thought I'd lost my best friend in the world." I could barely hear him he was so quiet.

Matt leaned in. "Tell me what happened after you left the party with Barb."

Tim glanced at Matt and then turned his body away towards the corner, his shoulders hunched.

"Tim. I need to know. Were you with Barb when she killed Julie?"

He whirled back around. "Barb didn't kill Julie. She was with me the whole night."

"Then how was her car spotted in front of Julie's house at 3:20 that morning?"

"What are you talking about?" He seemed genuinely surprised.

Matt showed him a picture of the day planner and then the photocopied image of the relevant page. "Ms. Franks, who lived across from Julie, noted down everything about her neighbors. What they wore, when they left the house, when they returned. And who parked in front of their house. She had a stroke the day Julie was found. But she'd recorded this entry before she did. See this?"

Tim stared at the page.

"That indicates that Barb's car was parked in front of Julie's house at 3:20 the morning she was killed. So I'll ask again, were you there when Barb killed Julie?"

He sagged forward like every bone in his body had just dissolved.

"Tim. Tell me what happened. Tell me which of you killed her. We do have enough to arrest you with this. Do you really want your children to go into foster care if they don't have to? You need to stop protecting her."

He shook his head slowly back and forth. "I never knew. But…All these years. No wonder…"

"No wonder what?"

"It makes so much sense now."

"So it *was* Barb?"

He shook his head again, still lost in his own world. "No. Not Barb."

Matt finally sat down. "Then who was it?"

Tim sort of laughed, but it was a wounded sound. "I think it was my mother."

CHAPTER TWENTY-EIGHT

I DEFINITELY HADN'T SEEN THAT COMING.

But as soon as he told Matt he thought it was his mother, Tim let everything out. Through sobs he explained that he and Barb had gone back to his house that night, but they hadn't tried to make up. It turns out that Tim had a bit of a routine when he was angry and upset. He'd pop a whole bunch of pills and talk about wanting to die until Barb convinced him to throw them back up. There were no medical records of it, because she always managed to convince him in time.

That night it had taken a little longer than normal and enough of the meds must've gotten into his system to make him especially woozy. He didn't quite pass out, but he was out enough to not really be aware of what was going on around him.

He said he had vague memories of his mother coming home that night, drunk. He'd thought at the time that she was mad at Barb and screaming and shouting about how Barb had ruined his life. But looking back on it now, he realized that his mother must've been talking about Julie.

His mother didn't have a working car. She bummed rides to and from work with co-workers or neighbors. And to and from the bar with "friends". So she must've taken Barb's SUV that night and gone over to confront Julie. Because he did clearly remember Barb being there with him the whole night.

After he finished, he bent over clutching his stomach. "I can't believe...All these years. They both knew and..."

Matt patted him on the shoulder and left him alone in the interview room to come find me.

"What do you think?" I asked as we both stood there in that cramped, too hot space and watched Tim rock back and forth on the computer monitor, sobbing.

"It rings true to me."

"Me, too."

"But now I have to convince Barb to tell us what happened that night. Because it's still just conjecture and guesswork at this point. We still don't have a case."

I nodded. We didn't have one yet, but we would. I knew Matt would get the story out of her.

Unfortunately, we had to wait a few hours to actually interrogate Barb because she was clearly drunk when the cops brought her in. (Tim had come alone and we'd let him because of the kids. But seeing the state she was in, I sure hoped that babysitter had been around, too.)

By the time she finally blew a number below the legal limit I was on Coke number five for the day and ready to be done already.

Matt sat down across from her. "Do you know why we're here, Barb?"

She sneered at him. "Julie Lewis. I told you we left that party and that was the last I ever saw her."

"But you know who killed her."

She shook her head. "No I don't. Tim and I went to his mom's and that's where we stayed the whole night."

"That's not how Tim tells it."

She laughed, once. "And what does he say? Because as I recall that night he was mostly passed out, wasn't he?"

Matt leaned forward. "He wasn't so passed out that he missed you and his mom having a fight."

"So we yelled at each other. That wasn't anything new. She thought he could do better than me. She didn't want her baby boy tied down at such a young age. She thought he could go pro if only he wasn't distracted by me."

"But that's not what you were fighting about that night, is it?"

Barb crossed her arms and rolled her eyes. "It's been years. I can't remember the conversation."

Matt pulled out his photocopy of the journal entry from Ms. Franks. "Do you know what this is?"

"No."

"It turns out Julie's elderly neighbor had insomnia. And she liked to write down every single visitor that came to Julie's house."

"So?"

"So this record says that it was your vehicle that was at Julie's house that night."

"Well, duh. We picked her up for the party."

"At three in the morning?"

Barb leaned forward and looked at the license plate number that was clearly visible on the page.

She shrugged one shoulder. "It wasn't me."

"Who was it? Who did you give your vehicle to?"

She shook her head, but refused to answer.

Matt leaned forward and fixed her with a glare. "I have to admit Barb, you don't strike me as the best mom in the world. But I'd hate to see those kids of yours lose their mom for a crime she didn't commit."

"Exactly. I didn't do anything."

"You had material information relevant to a police investigation and you failed to disclose that information. You can go to jail for that. Unless you help me now. Tell me what you know. Who killed Julie Lewis?"

"If I tell you, do you promise to leave me out of it?"

"You'll have to testify. But I think we can probably leave it at that."

"Fine."

Barb crossed her arms, closed her eyes, leaned her head back, and told Matt everything she knew about that night.

According to her, Tim's mom had come home from the bar, seen him barely conscious, and started screaming at Barb about how she was ruining his life and was no good for him. Barb screamed right back and told her it was Julie's fault not hers that he'd taken the pills. And then she told her what had happened that night.

Tim's mom was furious. More furious than it warranted, in Barb's opinion. She demanded Barb's keys so she could go over there and tell that girl to stay away from her boy for once and for all.

Amused by the idea Barb had happily handed over the keys and went to curl up with Tim who was passed out in bed. She was asleep by the time Tim's mom returned. The next morning Barb found Tim's mom sitting in the kitchen, red-eyed like she'd never gone to bed.

She asked his mom what had happened the night before. According to Barb, his mom refused to tell her but did suggest that Barb clean up her vehicle before someone came by. When she went out to her SUV there was a bunch of mud on the wheels, so Barb started to hose it down. Tim's mom came out a minute or two later and took something wrapped in a rag out of the backseat. Barb didn't get a clear view of what it was, but she suspected it might be a tire iron.

She said she'd thought about driving by Julie's house or calling to see if she was okay, but she hadn't. Instead she'd stayed with Tim pretending everything was fine until Mr. Lewis called and told them that Julie had been killed. When the call came in and Tim started screaming, his mother had walked out of the house and hadn't come back until the next day.

Barb never spoke to Tim's mom about what happened that night. Never asked her why she'd done it. And never told anyone, not even Tim, what had happened. But as soon as she could, she got rid of the SUV. She gave it to Tim's mom out of spite. And to protect herself, just in case anyone ever came looking.

"Do you feel sorry for what happened to Julie?" Matt asked.

Barb shrugged and looked away. "She was my friend. But she was also going to take everything I'd ever wanted away from me."

He left her there, staring into the corner of the room, her face completely blank.

CHAPTER TWENTY-NINE

WE DROVE BACK FROM SALINA IN SILENCE FOR THE FIRST couple of hours. I hadn't even remembered to start up my iPod, so it was literally silent except for the slush of the snow against my van's tires and the occasional thwack of the wiper blades.

Matt held my hand as I drove. And I held his. We needed that connection. That tie to something good. Something pure.

Because the death of Julie Lewis was just one big tragedy that could've been avoided in so many ways. That poor girl, everything had gone wrong for her that night. She'd never had that chance to grow up, to make mistakes and find love. To travel and explore and grow and see life in all its many aspects.

And worst of all, we still didn't really know why.

The next day Matt arrested Tim's mom. I sat in the viewing room as he led her into interrogation. She was a tiny woman, probably not even five-two, but she had a wiry strength to her. This was a woman who'd been knocked down by life and come back up swinging. Her voice when she finally spoke was the gravelly voice of a lifetime smoker.

"Do you know why you're here?" Matt asked as he settled into the seat across from her.

"Tim called last night. Told me you'd talked."

"So you want to tell me what happened?"

She met Matt's gaze, but didn't answer.

If she didn't confess, I wasn't sure we'd have a case. I mean maybe we could prove it. Use Barb's testimony, but a drunk bitter woman didn't strike me as the best witness in the world. And we wouldn't be able to use the entry from Ms. Parks.

When it became clear she wasn't going to speak, Matt leaned forward. "You know the part I don't get? Why? I mean, what had Julie Lewis ever done to you? Or to Tim? Every single person we talked to said they were close friends. That they were good for each other. So why kill her?"

"Do you have kids?" she asked.

"No."

"Then you wouldn't understand."

"Explain it to me. Please."

He held her gaze until she finally looked away. "Did you know, I had Tim when I was seventeen?"

Matt nodded and waited for her to continue.

"My parents kicked me out when they found out I was pregnant. I went to the father, but he wanted nothing to do with it. I had plans, you know. I was going to move to LA, become an actress. But I didn't, did I? I stayed in this worthless place, gave up all my dreams. All for him. For my boy."

I studied her in confusion, still not understanding why

she'd done what she had. Matt, being the good cop he was, didn't say anything.

Finally, she continued. "I didn't like Barb much. I worried he'd get her pregnant and that would be that, but I figured he'd outgrow her after high school. Sure, they were going to go to the same college, because she was that kind of girl, but I figured he'd get there and he'd see all the other girls on campus and he and Barb would be over by Christmas. In time for him to really start focusing on baseball and make something of himself. He had potential, you know? Lots of potential."

Matt nodded, but still didn't speak.

"But Julie. When Barb told me what had happened that night. That he'd confessed his love to her and she'd rejected him and he'd tried to kill himself. I knew he'd never outgrow that. He'd always pine for Julie. Always want her. And she'd ruin his life. So I went over there to tell her to stay away from him."

"Why'd you leave her house?"

"I didn't know where her dad was. I wanted to have a one-on-one conversation without him around. He was always the type to step in and defend people like that," she said. "So I told her Tim was really sick and upset and needed to see her. I begged her to come with me."

"And she went?"

She nodded.

"Did you mean to kill her?"

She met his eyes for a long moment and then looked away.

"Ms. Holt? Did you mean to kill her?"

She shrugged her shoulders.

"Why the turnout?"

"It was close, it was private. I figured I could say what needed saying without anyone to interrupt."

"And then you went back home."

She nodded. "And then I went back home."

He leaned forward. "What did you do with the tire iron?"

"Trash."

"Are you sorry for what you did?" he asked.

She laughed softly. "You know, I was trying to look after my boy. Keep him from making the same mistake I did. But Julie's death drove him right to Barb. No way he was going to give her up after all they'd been through together. He never even played one season of baseball in college because of her."

"I met their kids. They're cute. And he's got a good job. He's a teacher."

She looked at Matt, her eyes dead. "Yeah, but he could've gone pro."

I turned away. I'd seen enough. It was time to tell Mr. Lewis who'd killed his daughter. And why.

CHAPTER THIRTY

I MET MR. LEWIS AT HIS HOUSE. HE INVITED ME IN AND we sat in that living room of his with all the pictures on the wall of Julie.

"Did you find the killer?" he asked me, lacing the fingers of his large hands together as he sat on the edge of the couch, every line of his body taut with tension.

"We did."

His knuckles went white as he clutched his hands tighter together. "Who was it? Who killed my little girl?"

"Melody Holt. Tim's mom."

He stared at me. "Why? Did she say?"

"She said it was because she thought Julie was going to ruin his life. That he wouldn't pursue baseball if he fell in love with Julie. Honestly, it didn't make a lot of sense to me."

"That's because you never saw Melody and John."

"John?"

"Tim's father." He shook his head. "Melody was an amazing actress. When she talked about moving to LA everyone agreed that they'd see her on the big screen some-day. But then she fell for John. He was horrible to her. He knew she loved him, but he was always hanging around other girls or saying horrible things about Melody to his friends. Didn't keep him from sleeping with her, of course. When she ended up pregnant, John cut off all ties. Said the baby wasn't his. Left for college and never looked back."

"But why kill a girl over that?"

"Melody had big dreams. Dreams that John took away from her. Dreams she placed on her son. And Julie…I can see how she'd remind Melody of John." He grimaced. "I loved my girl, but sometimes she treated Tim the way John treated Melody. Just took for granted that he was there for her and always would be. Didn't give back to him what he gave to her."

"I'm so sorry, Mr. Lewis."

He reached over and squeezed my hand. "Don't be. You found my daughter's killer. Something I never thought would happen. Thank you."

"You're welcome." I gave him back Julie's diary. "I think you should read this again. I know you probably saw all the times she was angry with you the first time you read it. But I hope if you read it again that you also see what I saw, which is how close you were and how much she loved you and knew what a great father you were."

I gave him a quick hug and left before I started crying. It was hard to be reminded of what it was like to have a parent that loved you that much. I had Matt now and my grandpa and the friends I'd found along the way, but nothing in life could ever compare to having parents who truly cared for you. I'd lost my parents when I was too young, but I would always have their love with me. It was the most precious gift they'd ever given me and something no one could take away.

CHAPTER THIRTY-ONE

SPRING IN THE COLORADO MOUNTAINS. I'D LIKE TO SAY that the birds were singing and the flowers were blooming and that it was a balmy sixty-degrees Fahrenheit, but this was Colorado in the mountains in the middle of March. Which meant that the first day of spring was forty degrees with a few inches of snow on the ground.

I was bumbling around the kitchen, dreading Fancy's daily walk when my grandpa strolled through, nuked himself up the leftover coffee from the day before, and poured it into a travel mug.

"Where are you headed this early?" I asked.

"Out."

I frowned at him. "Out? Out to where? It's six-thirty in the morning."

"I know."

"I thought we were having breakfast this morning. You told me to wait for you."

He winked at me and glanced out the window. "My mistake. Guess you'll have to have breakfast with Matt instead."

I'd known it was the day Matt was going to propose, but I'd thought he'd do it that night not before the sun was even up. I expected to freeze in panic, but I didn't. I was actually kind of sort of looking forward to it. The investigation of Julie Lewis's death had changed me. In a good way.

I followed my grandpa to the door and waited for Matt to walk up the front walk.

"Happy first day of spring," he said, looking slightly nervous. "I brought you this."

It was a bright yellow tulip in a small green pot.

"I know you don't like flowers because they just die, but I figured this one would be okay because it's potted."

"It's beautiful, thank you," I said, feeling teary for some inexplicable reason.

I glanced down the street and saw Lucas Dean coming out of his house. He was not going to be a part of my special moment, no siree.

I stepped inside, pushing Fancy out of the way, as I walked towards the kitchen. "Come on, come inside before you freeze. I was just about to cook breakfast. My grandpa asked me to wait for him last night, but I guess it was just one big bait and switch, huh? You guys had this whole thing planned out in advance? Well, I hope you like bacon and eggs, because that's what's on the menu."

I would've kept blubbering on, but I turned back at the kitchen doorway to see Matt kneeling on one knee. He would be a traditionalist, wouldn't he?

My throat went dry. I desperately wished I had a Coke in my hand. Or even water. Or maybe vodka. Lots and lots of vodka.

He held his hand out towards me and I stepped towards him, but Fancy beat me to the punch. You don't kneel down on the level of a dog that big without her thinking it's about her. She started licking his face like crazy and wagging her tail and jumping around.

I burst out laughing. "Fancy. Stop it. Go on. Get away. Shoo." I shoved her towards the kitchen. "Go outside."

She ducked me and went back towards Matt. He stood up, laughing, too. "Well, I expect if you're not into all the other trappings you won't mind if I do this while standing?"

"Not at all" I said, softly, afraid I was going to burst into tears at any moment.

He pulled a small red ring box out of his jeans pocket. His hand was trembling. I wanted more than anything to reach out and cover it with mine, but I didn't. I pressed my fist to my lips and waited.

He met my eyes. "Maggie May Carver, will you marry me?"

He opened the box.

The ring inside was perfect. (For me.) It had a band each of white gold and rose gold entwined together and engraved with roses. No big stone to get caught in my hair for the rest of my life. No gaudy amount of diamonds to make me wonder if he'd blown all his money. Just a simple symbol of our love.

"It's beautiful." I smiled at him, tears in the corner of my eyes. "You remembered."

"I did. So? What's your answer?"

I laughed. "Oh, right. Of course. I have to actually answer."

He nodded and looked at me, waiting.

"Yes. Yes, I'll marry you. Of course I will."

He pulled me into a big hug and spun me around in a circle, which caused Fancy to go absolutely crazy and start barking at us very loudly.

"Shush, Fancy," I said when he finally set me down. But then he kissed me and I pretty much forgot the entire world for a moment. How was I lucky enough to have found such an amazing man?

"You want to try it on?" he asked when he was done taking my breath away.

"Try on what?"

"The ring."

"Oh, right. Yeah. Sorry. I'm just a little flustered, that's all. No food, no Coke, and a wedding proposal. I'm not quite in my right mind."

"Well, let's take care of that, shall we? One Coke coming up and then I am going to make you the best cream cheese stuffed waffles you've ever had."

"I thought you couldn't cook?" I said, following him into the kitchen where he pulled an almost perfectly frozen Coke out of the freezer. (He and my grandpa had definitely been conspiring on this one.)

He winked. "I've been practicing. Jamie's been giving me lessons. She said you really like a man who can cook."

"That is definitely true. Although I was willing to over-look it for you."

"No need." He kissed me on the cheek and pushed me towards the kitchen table while he whipped up the most delicious looking breakfast I'd ever had.

I took a sip of my Coke and slid the ring on my finger. It fit perfectly. As I admired it, I said, "I'm going to have to call Jamie. She probably already knew you were going to propose, but I should tell her I said yes. Oh, and my grandpa, too."

Matt gave me an odd look. "Actually...Speaking of that..."

"What?"

"Well, you did say you wanted things to happen fast, right? You didn't want to spend a lot of time and energy on preparing for a wedding."

I nodded, suddenly nervous.

"Well, if you really meant it, I thought we could get married today."

It's a good thing I hadn't just taken a sip of my Coke or I would've spit it out. "Today?" I squeaked.

He tensed and nodded. "Yeah. What do you think?"

I blinked as I tried to get my brain back into working order. "Um."

I glanced out the window. "Where were you thinking we'd have it? Because my personal preference for getting married at the top of the canyon probably isn't going to work so well today what with all the snow."

"I know. And..." He winced. "Don't be mad at me, please..."

"About what?"

"I know your ideal wedding is just the two of us on the side of a mountain."

I nodded. "In theory."

"But your grandpa said there was no way his grand-daughter was getting married in the town he lives in without him there."

"Okay, that's fine. I would kind of like to have him there."

He stepped closer, still looking like he expected me to lose it at any moment. "And of course that means Lesley."

I was starting to see where this was going. "Right..."

"And Jack said he better be invited, too. I mean, he is my brother."

"Which means Trish and Sam."

He nodded.

"And I expect Jamie and Mason want to be there, too?"

He nodded again. "And Greta. And Jean-Philippe. And Evan and Abe. And if we're going that far..."

I sighed. "You have friends and co-workers who'll want to be there, too."

He nodded.

I sat back, my visions of a quiet intimate promise between just me and Matt suddenly blown to bits. Then again, there wasn't a single person he'd listed that I wasn't willing to have there.

He sat down across from me and took my hand. "We can still have the wedding you want, just the two of us. All I care about is getting married to you. Today or when the snow actually thaws or whenever. And wherever. What matters is us, Maggie."

I sighed. "Well, now that you mentioned everyone, it does seem only fair to include them." I took a long sip of Coke. "It's just that I don't want to plan it. They're such a hassle and such an expense." I glanced at the living room. "Maybe we could just ask everyone to drop by this weekend and you know, say our vows or whatever."

"We could." He grinned at me. "Or, better yet, we could get married today at four o'clock and you could let those friends of yours, who love you very much, put the wedding plans they've been making into effect."

I raised my eyebrows. "Wedding plans they've been making?"

"They have it all. The flowers, the venue, the guests, the dresses, the food. All I have to do is make one phone call and it happens." He held up his phone. "So? What do you say? Are we going to do this thing or not?"

I bit my lip, feeling one last shiver of fear. This was it.

This was the make or break moment. "Go ahead. Let's do this. On one condition."

"What's that?"

"We invite Mr. Lewis, too."

Matt nodded. "Already done."

EPILOGUE

AT FOUR O'CLOCK ON THE FIRST DAY OF SPRING IN THE small Colorado mountain town of Creek I found myself standing in front of a red wooden door wearing a beautiful sapphire blue dress with a fitted bodice and long skirt that flared from my hips but wasn't poofy. (The one I'd tried on and borrowed at Greta's for Jamie's wedding if you remember.)

Because it was cold out, I also had a (fake) white fur wrap around my shoulders and matching blue snow boots on my feet. (It was nice to know my friends knew me well enough to know I'd refuse to wear skinny little heels.)

That red door belonged to the house next door to my grandpa's, the one Matt and I were going to move into that day, immediately after the ceremony.

Matt hadn't bought the house, thankfully—marriage and joint property ownership on the same day would've been just a little too much for me—but he had arranged to rent it for three months with an option to buy if we liked it.

My friends had transformed the place into a magical (and warm) winter wonderland with a gigantic tent in the backyard and thousands of little white lights strung everywhere.

I hadn't had to do a thing but show up. Matt and I ran to the courthouse first thing to get our marriage license and then Jamie and Greta whisked me away for a day of prepping and pampering which involved lots of yummy finger foods (courtesy of Jean-Philippe) and probably a few too many Bellinis.

It made for a nice relaxing day even if I had been forced to sit through hair and make-up. The make-up took an inordinately long time because the woman kept stepping back from doing my eyes and saying, "Oh, look at that, how gorgeous," every few minutes. Honestly, it looked good when it was done, but not one hour of my life good. But, hey, I was being accommodating so I just let it happen.

Thankfully the woman who did my hair kept the hairspray within manageable limits. She took small sections from the front on each side and braided them back and then let the rest of my hair fall loose and curled down my back. (It was long at that point, too. I hadn't realized I'd grown it out as much as I had.) She then tucked in matching blue, lavender, and white baby roses through the braided sections, gave it a small bit of spray, and that was it. Not too bad. Something I could live with.

Jamie and Greta were my bridesmaids. They had long lavender dresses that complemented my dress perfectly. And matching lavender boots, which made me laugh. (Something I desperately needed as the moment of reckoning drew closer.)

When it was finally time, we hopped into a limo and drove over to the house.

It had been transformed. No longer was it a small ranch-style house in need of a good paint job. Now it was covered in little white lights that gave it a charming fairy-tale sort of feel.

I stopped in front of the door, scared to go inside. This was it. This was the end. Or the beginning. Or just one more day along the continuum. A day that could be just like any other except for how scared I felt.

I didn't want to get this wrong. Not the wedding. If I got the wedding wrong we'd just have something to laugh at for the next fifty years. No, it was life with Matt I didn't want to get wrong. I swore to myself in that moment I would try the best I could to make him happy.

Before my thoughts could spiral towards how hard that was going to be, Jamie pinched me. "Enough. Go inside. We're freezing out here."

"But…"

"Maggie, if I have to grab you by the ear, drag you inside, and force you to say these vows, I will. Don't doubt it." Since Jamie is normally the most laid back of people her vehemence surprised me, but it had its intended effect. I opened the door and stepped inside.

It smelled delicious. I'd expected French cuisine because of Jean-Philippe, but that's not what I smelled. "Is that…?"

"Yep." Jamie squeezed my hand. "Your grandpa made some of your dad's green chili, your grandma's pinto beans, and your mom's homemade tortillas."

I instantly wanted to cry. Happy-sad tears, knowing they couldn't be there to see me get married but would be there in spirit through their signature dishes.

"You can't tell me that right before the wedding," I wailed. "I'm going to cry all my makeup off." I stared at the ceiling and blinked rapidly for ten seconds to keep the tears from falling.

"Sorry. I forget because you're not usually one to cry."

"Yeah, well, when the tears come, they really come, so let's try to get through the ceremony before that happens, shall we?"

My grandpa stepped into the living room just then. He was wearing a black tuxedo with a lavender cummerbund and looked downright dapper.

"Grandpa." I gave him a quick hug. "Thank you. Jamie told me about the green chili, pinto beans, and tortillas."

He gave me an extra squeeze. "You're welcome. I figured that was the best way to have them be part of the day with us." His voice was rough as he said it.

"Don't you start crying or I'm never going to be able to hold it together," I told him.

He wiped a tear from his eye. "Okay. No more tears. This is a happy day. For both of us."

I probably would've just broken down into tears at that point, but fortunately Jack, Trish, and Sam arrived.

"Maggie, Maggie, Maggie," Sam cried running over to me with a big grin on his freckled face. He was in a little tuxedo himself, the lavender of his bow tie a perfect complement for his red hair. "Guess what?"

"What?" I asked, smiling at his enthusiasm.

"I'm your ring bearer. And I get to ride Lady down the aisle."

That definitely cleared up any lingering desire to cry. I turned to Jack who gave me a wicked grin. (He was as tall, dark, and handsome as Matt but I'd always had the feeling that kissing him would be like taking one gigantic step down the path to ruin.)

I stalked over to him. "Lady? Is this the Lady I think it is?"

"If you mean the incredibly well-behaved and docile miniature horse, Lady, then yes."

I crossed my arms. "You're telling me that there's going to be a miniature horse at my wedding."

He winked. "That's what you get for not wanting to plan your own wedding."

I glanced over at Jamie who shrugged back at me. "It seemed like a fun idea at the time."

I closed my eyes and took a deep breath, reminding myself that if it went wrong it was a funny story to tell. The only thing we had to get right was Matt and I exchanging our vows. That was it. That was all that had to happen. Matt and I promising to be together forever.

I frowned. "What about Fancy? If Lady is going to be in the wedding, then Fancy should be, too."

Jack grinned at Jamie. "Told you."

"So you did." Jamie nodded. "Fancy will be in the wedding if you want her to be. Matt found her a matching leash and collar. And, um…"

"What? What now?"

"Jack found a groomer who temporarily dyed the tops of her ears blue."

Yep, definitely no lingering desire to cry at that point. "You dyed my dog's ears blue? Let me see her," I snapped.

Jack left and came back with Fancy on a sapphire blue leash that matched my dress and with the hair on the tops of each ear dyed blue. I had to admit, the ears actually looked pretty cute. And Fancy certainly didn't seem to notice the difference. Plus she wouldn't be able to shake it off like she would've if they'd tried to put bows on her.

She was also wearing her Go-Pro camera harness. "Didn't I mention?" Jack asked. "She's the official wedding videographer, too."

Before I could lose it, Jamie gently touched my arm and pointed to where an actual videographer was walking around capturing footage of the event. "But not the only one," she said.

I nodded and took a deep breath. Okay. It was unorthodox, but no denying it was also just the right type of wedding for me. (And Matt. Couldn't forget Matt.)

"What do you think, Fancy? You ready to do this thing?" I asked her.

She looked around the room at everyone and then yawned and laid down. Leave it to a dog to put things in perspective. It was just another day. A lot more going on, but just another day.

So I told myself until they opened the back door and I caught a glimpse of Matt standing at the front of the crowd in a tuxedo with a bright blue cummerbund that matched my dress and his eyes, a flower-covered arch festooned with white lights and blue, purple, and white roses behind him.

He was gorgeous.

And scared.

And then he saw me. And he smiled, a smile so bright it hurt. And those frickin' tears came back and threatened to overwhelm me.

"Let's get this over with," I said.

Not that I meant it in *that* way, but we only had so long before I was going to completely lose it and as I'd already told Matt, I do not pretty cry.

As Trish helped Sam onto Lady—whose bridle matched my dress and who had flowers woven into the little braids in her mane—Jack came over to me. "He's the best guy you could ever hope to marry. You know that, right?"

I nodded. "I wouldn't be marrying him otherwise."

"If you ever break his heart, I'll steal your dog."

I laughed and glanced down at Fancy. "My dog? What kind of threat is that?"

He shrugged. "I figured I'm good at stealing things. And aside from Matt, Fancy and your grandpa are the two things you love most in this world. I'm pretty sure if I tried to steal your grandpa, he'd shoot me. So Fancy it is."

I laughed again, my tears once more banished for the moment. "How about this. I won't break his heart, you don't need to steal anything, and we all have our happily ever after. Deal?"

"Deal."

Greta came over. I knew she'd wanted me to marry someone rich and old for my first husband and save Matt for a later marriage, but she squeezed my hand and said in her German accent, "He will make a good husband for you, Maggie, I know it."

"So do I. Thank you."

Jack held his arm out to her and they walked out the doorway as the sound of some sort of beautiful music played in the background. Mason and Jamie followed right behind.

And then it was my turn.

My grandpa handed me a bouquet of lavender, blue, and white roses and held his arm out for me. "You're making the right choice, Maggie."

"I know." And I did. Matt was exactly the right man for me. I didn't expect it to be perfect—life never is—but if there was anyone I wanted to tie my life to and let change me in ways I couldn't even foresee, it was Matt.

As I stopped in the doorway I saw Abe and Evan, their skin nicely tanned from their vacation. Mr. Lewis, his eyes already full of tears. Elaine, sitting quietly by herself in the back. Lesley, as polished as ever in a darker purple dress that complemented the colors of the wedding. Jean-Philippe who gave me an entirely inappropriate up and down appraisal and then winked at me. Matt, waiting nervously. Jack, standing at his side with a roguish grin. Mason, all serious and sober next to him. And Greta and Jamie beaming smiles at me.

These were my friends.

My family.

I'd always thought that I wouldn't want to go through my wedding day because it would be too painful without my parents there. But looking around at all those faces I realized that even though some of the people I'd loved most in this world couldn't be there that day that I still had plenty of love in my life.

I hadn't come to Creek looking for this, but I was glad I'd found it. And I'd be forever grateful for the twisted, crazy path that had brought me here.

I took a deep breath and stepped forward, a smile on my face, my grandpa and Fancy by my side, to start my next big adventure.

ABOUT THE AUTHOR

When Aleksa Baxter decided to write what she loves it was a no-brainer to write a cozy mystery set in the mountains of Colorado where she grew up and starring a Newfie, Miss Fancypants, that is very much like her own Newfie, in both the good ways and the bad.

You can reach her at aleksabaxterwriter@gmail.com or on her website aleksabaxter.com.

To hear about new releases or promotions, sign up for her mailing list.

CPSIA information can be obtained
at www.ICGtesting.com
Printed in the USA
FSHW021830120420
69097FS